# AM

# MY

# SISTER'S

# KEEPER

Author

## KILENE 'KI' WILLIAMS

Publisher: Bleeding Ink Creatives, LLC

Book Cover Photography by: Dezhomme Photography / Dezhomme Enterprises

Book Cover Model: Brittney Nugent

# I AM MY SISTER'S KEEPER

## Copyright 2019 © Kilene Williams

## *DEDICATION*

First, I dedicate this book to the readers. Thank you for reading *I Am My Sister's Keeper*. Your time and attention are humbly appreciated.

I too dedicate this book to myself for finally having the courage to pour my heart into my first love, writing. I have always wanted to become a fiction author and share the stories in my heart and psyche with the world. This is only the beginning.

Thank you for reading!

# Chapter One - Victoria

It can't be time to wake up already. I feel as if my head just hit the pillow. "Sweet awakenings my sunshine. I pray you rested well." Pierre whispered in my ear softly. I tried to breathe as shallow as possible unwilling to acknowledge the echoes piercing my need for just a little more silence. Sleep. Gently kissing the nape of my neck, I moaned and smiled giving in to the shine seeping through the darkness. We kiss, and our good morning begins.

Clearing my throat, I looked up at Pierre and responded, "I slept well dear, but you know I'm always trying to stay undercovers for as long as possible in the mornings. I am going to put the coffee on. Please start the shower for me." "I already have, you know I'm always two thoughts ahead of you."

Confidence rolling off Pierre's tongue, I hear him laughing just loud enough for me to notice as I was walking back from the kitchen. "That's why I love you, for always knowing what I need. Speaking of needs, can you please run into the store after work this evening to pick up a couple bags of Timex. I just brewed the last of what we had, and our day cannot start without it. I may overdose with my designs due at the end of the week. If Fredricka does not approve four of the six, I am done. Finished." Gasping for air, my eyes lower to the smile on Pierre's lips, he is the essence of calm while my mind explodes. Pulling me close Pierre mouths, "*breathe.*"

"Pierre, I've laid out my choices for today's board meeting across the bed. Which is your pick? I'm going back to pour our coffee. Grab my journal on your way to the kitchen. Breakfast will be ready in a minute." One cup of mixed berries (blueberries, strawberries and raspberries), two egg whites, one fresh tomato sliced thinly, sautéed spinach and a tall glass of my famous fresh squeezed lemon, lime orange juice is our fuel for the morning.

Gazing into Pierre's eyes I could see the joy in his heart shining. It was as if he was up to something and couldn't wait to surprise me. His demeanor always shifts to this dazed look when he plans to surprise me, and my stomach immediately flutters when he looks at me this way. It's almost as if he is seeing through me.

Pierre's dark chocolate eyes light up my soul. His perfect lips full to perfection softly pull me in. We are the same complexion with similar features around the nose and mouth area. We always laugh and say our love made us look alike. I remember my grandmother used to say, *if you feed a person long enough, they will start to look like you.* We definitely keep each other well fed. I love my handsome 6'1" 195 pounds of lean fineness intoxicated with intelligence. Listening to him speak makes me wet and he loves every drip of it. I can't wait to see him rocking the new Italian custom tailored suit he had made for our anniversary evening.

Smiling as I hand over his plate, Pierre gave his opinion. "You should wear the white dress with the royal blue coat, shoes and brief case." "Thanks dear, I knew you'd say that. I will save the pink dress for dinner this evening. Don't forget we have reservations. I cannot wait to celebrate our sixth wedding anniversary. It seems like we've already spent a lifetime together. I love you Pierre." "My sweet Victoria, I wish only to spend eternity in your arms."

The base in Pierre's voice sent warm-blooded chills through my body, kissing my forehead gently, he began to lead me towards our room. "This morning, my beautiful wife we are going to do things a little different. I will wash your every inch and make love to you again and again." Sending moans through my soul I let out a deep seeded sigh foreseeing orgasmic bliss, thinking yes, as you wish.

Pierre grabbed me by the waist stepping into the steamy shower, our bodies intertwined, I lean my head just backwards letting the heat of the water massage my scalp as Pierre runs his hands through my hair feverishly. Love dripping from his lips as we kiss, passionately, my legs clench tighter as my center opens wider. Running my fingers down the center of his chest, I only have one request - before

I can finish, I find myself breathless. His love penetrates deeply, always knowing exactly how to please me. Kissing me as he brings my body down slowly, making my thoughts melt and my heart smile.

"I love you Victoria." "I love you too Pierre." He washed my body from head to toe, gently smacked me on the ass, and watched me walk away.

Our ceilings being higher than most, makes our bathroom a piece of heaven. Our shower has a sky dome with a clear finish allowing us to look up and see the stunning trees and beautiful sunrises, sunsets and midday hues of the sky's baby blues. Taking  all of this in while we enjoy the many features of the state-of-the-art shower head I handpicked is bliss.

"Pierre, what is on your agenda for today?  I am so proud of you for giving yourself designated time off from work to regroup. You have been burning at both ends, and I don't want you to burn out. So many young people under fifty are dying every day from heart attacks, strokes and other diseases that could be avoided with proper balance of life and health. You promised me forever my king, and I intend to hold you to it. As an entrepreneur, I know there is very little time to rest, but if you don't take proper care of yourself, you can't profess to be here for the ones you love." "You're right my queen, you're right."

"Pierre, will you help me zip up my dress please? Thank you. I will see you this evening." I winked at Pierre as I caught his dreamy eyes admiring my frame from head to toe. "You look stunning my love." Pierre's voice was deep, and smooth like milk chocolate melting in your mouth. He continued. "Make sure you have everything you need. Meet me at the condo after work. We will freshen up and change there.

Our car will be picking us up for dinner at 7:30 this evening. Our reservations are for 8:15 this evening. I am going to the gym this morning, then to take a run on the shore and I also have a few other errands to finish, *like pick up your anniversary surprise.* I will be at the condo waiting for you this evening. Now get going before you drown in traffic, tell Sade hello for me this morning and kiss my beautiful niece and nephew. I love you Victoria." "I love you too Pierre, I can't wait for this evening."

When we first got married, Pierre and I bought a condo on Fort Lauderdale Beach. On the sixteenth floor, we enjoyed our two bedroom, two bathroom ocean front piece of heaven. It was always a dream of both of ours to own a place on the beach. So, before buying our own home with a yard for our future children and grandchildren, we decided to work a little backwards. It was the most exhilaratingly passionate purchase we had made. It is our little stay-cation get away.

After living in the condo for almost three years we both decided we wanted to move into a home in Wynwood. The Wynwood area of Miami was a perfect fit for our personalities. On our third wedding anniversary, we closed on our home. There are two guest homes on the property so I made one into a relaxing retreat for our family and friends when they come to visit, and the other into a home office for Pierre and myself.

In our home office, I decorated the loft and set up my first home art studio for my framed writings, sketches and books. I had floor to ceiling book shelves on three of the walls and a huge window facing east on the fourth wall which I left completely uncovered. Soundproof, it was my space to escape and be creatively immersed in making my dreams reality.

Downstairs was clean and crisp contemporary décor. It is a welcoming environment for Pierre as a trader to meet with his clients and work productively. With gold accent pillows perfectly placed, his appreciation for very little glam is embraced. We each have private entrances to avoid disturbing the other when working, unless there's an emergency. We have always respected each other's needs personally and professionally.

I am the Owner and Chief Executive Officer of Artistry, an organization that I created to motivate and empower creative people to become knowledgeable, confident individuals setting goals and taking action in life both personally and professionally. Our membership has grown tremendously with just one year of service under our belt. I am excited to share expansion details at this afternoon's board meeting.

Currently we offer voice lessons and music lessons for trumpet, saxophone, drums, piano, violin, cello and guitar. We have a phenomenal art teacher that offers various painting and drawing classes. We also have a writing circle for writers that includes insight into publishing and copyright understanding. All writers are welcome and our classes are purposely set up by age range and preferred genre. Local published authors are constantly donating their time and joy for writing in various seminars to support the writers within Artistry. The Wynwood community has been extremely supportive of our business and I am looking forward to marketing our newest changes and opportunities available to the community.

I have a few hours before I need to be present for the board meeting. We will be meeting this afternoon at Capital Grill downtown Fort Lauderdale at one o'clock sharp. I reserved the private dining room for the meeting. I have seven dedicated board members, and I value their insight, each for their unique perspective.

I am headed to visit with my sister Sade this morning before the meeting. She is the Economics and Finance expert on the board of Artistry. Sade just gave birth to twins, a boy and girl, Leo and Lea. Leo is sixteen minutes older than Lea. Odd I know, I have heard of twins generally being born a few minutes apart, but not sixteen minutes apart. Both healthy and gorgeous little blessings, I have to be the proudest aunt ever. Leo, 7 pounds and Lea 6.5 pounds were born on my birthday, July 30. I was overjoyed with happiness when my sister asked me to be their godmother. I am humbled and honored. I will always be here to provide and protect them both while empowering them with the tools necessary to survive in this world. She has just returned home with the twins and we all try to be there to pitch in at least once a day if not more. My mother, or my Sophia as I call her, has flown in from Manhattan to spend the first three months with her. During this time we are all a part of the interviewing process for a live in nanny.

My sister is a professor of Economics at the University of Miami in Coral Gables, Florida. She has taken six months leave of absence to be home and enjoy her beautiful babies. After six months she will return to her first born, Economics. I always love coming to visit my sister. Coral Gables is such a beautiful city.

Sade's husband, Joshua, has been missing since June 19. We are all trying to remain positive and prayerful of his safe return for my sister's sake. It has been over a month and Sade has yet to hear his voice.

When he left for Dubai on June 10, He called to let the family know he arrived safely. There have been no new updates to his missing person's case. The last time my sister heard his voice was the night before she thought he was to return home. She still hangs on to his last words, *"I love you,"* while she prays for him to walk through the door. I begged her to stay with us until he returned since she had the twins, but she refused. She wanted to be home when Joshua returned.

I have begun my own investigation into his disappearance after feeling like the local authorities are not as committed to finding him. Thirty-five years old and healthy. He had a full physical and screening before leaving the country. He seemed so happy about life and truly excited to meet his children. He and my sister have been married for three years, but like Pierre and I they dated for two and a half years before getting married. Best friends and lovers, is the only way to commit.

The police have said that there were no reports of accidents which include a man of his description and as of yet, none of his credit cards or other personal accounts have been used since June 18.

I realize my bluntness and hard exterior may seem harsh, but I think my sister's six months off will also help her come to grips with the fact that Joshua may never return, and we may never have answers. At least the time off will give her a chance to gain her strength so that she can get back to work and provide for my niece and nephew.

Sade and Joshua were inseparable. He a commercial real estate broker, and she an economic genius. Two beautiful nerds, a match made in heaven. It was always a fun time at Saturday dinners. We started having dinner every Saturday evening after she and Joshua got married. We wanted to start a new little family adult tradition. We all work so hard it required us to take out a few moments a week to be grateful and enjoy each other's company, no electronics allowed.

As I pull up I noticed mom's car was not in the driveway. She must have run to the store. I step out of the car with the biggest grin plastered on my face, it's what they do to me, I love staring into the twins eyes untainted by this life. The next generation, our future before us. My sister must have needed some fresh air. She was sitting on the front porch gazing at her garden while the twins were resting in their bassinet.

I loved her home. She chose a home with a gorgeous landscape. Since we were children my sister has always loved gardening. One day we will be able to eat all of our vegetables fresh from Sade's garden. The flowers brighten your day as soon as you turn into the driveway. Sunflowers, her favorite, adorned the walkway leading to the front door. She had created her small piece of paradise right at home. A very analytical soul, focused, driven and responsible, her garden lets her artistry flow freely.

"Hey auntie's, babies." The joy in my voice put a smile on the twins faces. "Good morning Sade. I am so excited about today sis. How are you? What is your pain level this morning? Have you had breakfast? Are you hungry? Where's mom?" "Good morning to you too Vic, wired much?

Which question would you like for me to answer first?" Sade began laughing hysterically. She loves to make fun of me when I am excited about my ideas coming to fruition. I tend to let my thoughts flow in overload, my wheels turning a mile a minute. "I love you sis, today is going to be great Victoria. I have already gone over the numbers repeatedly, the final proposal is stellar. I have every confidence that my little sister will walk away with board approval to move forward with the project." "Thank you Sade, your support means the world to me. I am honored that you agreed to sit on my board, and I appreciate every ounce of your constructive praise and criticism."

"I noticed mom's car was not here when I pulled in, where is she this early?" Sade answered with a hint of relief in her voice. "She started tennis lessons this week. Today is her first lesson. I'm so happy she is finding activities that she enjoys doing while here with us. She also swims for one hour three days a week. It is an excellent full body workout and gives her something to do just for herself. I guess mom hasn't had a chance to tell you that she has decided to stay for at least twelve months. I am not comfortable with hiring a nanny to be with the children solely. With mom here, she and I can take turns so there is always immediate family with them." "Oh wow! Sade that's wonderful, I am glad mom will be here, it's exciting. Since dad passed I have wanted to see her more and keep a closer watch on her health and happiness. This is such a blessing for you to have mom here hands on to help with our precious legacies. You know Pierre and I are here for you whenever you need also." I blew my big sis a kiss, and as always, she caught it in the palm of her hand and placed it over her heart.

"Well big sister are you hungry. I have a little time before the meeting." Sade's eyes lit up. "Yes, I took out some vegetables for mom to slice, season and sauté for me. Would you mind doing it?" "Of course I don't mind. I'll have a little myself so my stomach won't make desperate noises in hunger while I am presenting. I'll go in and get started right after I run and get your jar of my morning fresh squeezed lemon, lime orange juice out of the car." "Yes please Vic, you know it's my favorite." Sade has loved my morning, fresh squeezed concoction since I started making it. We were teenagers. I was working on eating healthier and loved working out. My juice was a refreshing treat. And of course my Sade enjoyed the benefits of my love for citrus fruits.

As I placed the jar of juice in the refrigerator to keep it cool while cooking, I heard my sister come into the house. "Sade, do you need me to help you bring the twins in." "No love, I got it. They are sleeping now so at least we have a few moments to enjoy each other and breakfast before you leave." I always loved one on one time with my sister. She is my favorite human. There is nothing I wouldn't do for her. Nothing.

"I don't want to upset you by asking, but have you heard from Joshua or received any updates. Have you checked his social media accounts again since last week? Have the police contacted you with any new information? I don't understand how someone vanishes in what seems to be thin air. Even more, I am shocked by how strong you've been through this entire ordeal." Taking a deep breath, I let out a loud sigh, and Sade began to speak in a matter-of-fact tone. "I love him Victoria, with all that is me, and I will never give in or give up on his safe return. I remain positive because it gives me the oxygen I need to breathe and remain present, healthy and nurturing to our babies." "Always know that I am here for you Sade. If you need to vent, celebrate, be silent or as loud as necessary, I am here. We got this!"

Pausing for a moment, I began to stare at the wedding picture mounted on the wall. Seeing the love in their eyes, brought tears to mine. Joshua towered over my sister by five inches. His blueish grey eyes caused a stillness in the room when he looked at you. I remember our last goodbye. Now looking at this portrait of forever hanging, I wonder why this is happening. The thin slither of his lips smiling reigns in my memories, recalling the day he promised my sister a lifetime of his loyalty, faithfulness and unconditional love.

"Sade, I'll be hunkering down this week. I need my designs ready for Ms. Fredricka by the end of the week. Of course everything is ready to go, but the designer in me is always adjusting and readjusting to the last second. If she is not impressed with at least four of the six I am expected to present, this opportunity is over for me. This will be huge for my fashion career, taking my sketches from art, to art flowing in motion." I could see Sade's eyes squinting as I explained. She waited patiently for me to finish. When she was sure I had said my peace, Sade jumped into big sister mode. "You know you will be six for six. Don't be intimated by her name or her brand. You were handpicked from Wynwood amateur fashion week for your amazing designs. You are the new face of Ms. Fredricka's brand, Lions clothing. Claim it, own it and know it sis! You are the epitome of what they stand for and your designs reflect their future. Class, grace and elegance with just the right hint of sexy and sass.

Besides, who else do you think is going to design the baby collection your niece and nephew will be modeling? Hello!" We both laughed and I hugged my sister with every ounce of love I had. "Thank you Sade, for being a positive, motivating and encouraging spirit. You are appreciated always."

"I am going to freshen up and get ready for my drive to Fort Lauderdale. I'm expected to arrive early to make sure the room is set up exactly as I need it before the first guest arrives." Early is always on time, therefore I require myself to be earlier than early to make sure every detail is in order. "Of course, no problem Vic. Try my new lipstick that I just received from our makeup consultant."

Our college best friend, Rae majored in Chemistry and is finally living her dreams. She started her own makeup line and opened up her first makeover spa in South Beach. She just bought a home in Sunny Isles and is truly doing amazing.

"Nice sis, I love it and you know I am so stealing this!" Sade laughed, having already predicted I would say that. "I knew you'd like it Vic, I kept it aside for you. Rae came by to check on me before I was discharged from the hospital and brought me a pampering bag of goodies. We should plan a beauty party, whiskey, bourbon and glam fun with our girls." My sister is right, we definitely need to get the girls together soon. "Yes, Rae and I will gladly plan a pampering day of fun to remember." Sade and I love Rae as if she was our triplet. We have been inseparable for years.

Normally mothers would be breastfeeding and unable to drink alcoholic beverages, however, Sade being a breast cancer survivor was unable to breastfeed for health reasons. She agonized over that reality for a long time before finally focusing on the best alternative she could come up with to provide her legacies.

A little rest, relaxation and libations with the girls is medicine for the soul. "I'll give Rae a call this weekend, Sade. She's always down for girl time, it helps to keep her from missing Stephen while he's gone." Rae's boyfriend, Stephen is a pilot and he travels often. He's an amazing ball of energy. His personality reminds me of Martin and Will combined from the Bad Boys movie series. Rae is truly in love with him, and we are in love with the way he treats her. A true gem, Stephen found a way to open up Rae's hard exterior and creep into the crevices of her heart.

"I love that we have similar taste. You're the best big sister in the world Sade! I've always wished we were twins. To me you are truly the most beautiful woman alive. Your gorgeous, flawless skin is life giving, and your beautiful honied glow lights up any room. At 5'9" you dear queen are every bit of runway material. Perfectly proportioned, my sister you are always the muse in my dreamy head when I am creating my designs. I am biased, always will be, but my big sister is EVERYTHING!" Sade was blushing when she interrupted. "Okay missy! Enough of all that considering most people can only tell us apart when I am standing and towering over you. I guess you're the most beautiful woman in the world too. Mirror images we are, whether you see it in yourself or not. The only difference between the two of us is age and height. Now, when you pop on those stilettos and take your 5'7" to 5'11" most don't know us apart. My precious little sister, our baby browns are one in the same. You are a gorgeous soul and I am honored to be your big sister. Now get your little ass out of here! It's time to make power moves." I always love when Sade showers me with her aggressive, positive energy.

"Okay Sade, what do you think? How do I look?" "You look like you are ready for a corporate take-over." Sade winked and struck a pose behind me in the mirror. We both smiled just the same and she watched as I ripped the runway all the way to the car. I am ready for what's next.

# Chapter Two - Sister Sister

When we were little Sade was the one that I could always expect to have my back in any situation. The first words I remember comprehending Sade whispering in my ear when she would sit and hold me in her narrow lap sooth my heart. *"You're my Victoria. I am my sister's keeper."*

A couple years my senior, Sade came equipped with big sister superpowers. She had a sixth sense when it came to my heart and emotions. She could tell something was going on with me whether good, bad or ugly. Our connection is surreal at times. The words, *I am my sister's keeper*, became our personal greeting, like hello or goodbye. Those words within each other's embrace were ethereal. Our bond has been unbreakable since inception.

I remember the first time she called to tell me about Joshua. I was so excited for Sade. I couldn't believe she finally decided that it was okay to give love a try again. Of course it wasn't love just yet, but for Sade to even mention her feelings about a man to me, means she's reached the point of no return. This gentleman, I thought, must be a gift from heaven to have my sister this enamored.

I know I sounded like mama, my Sophia, she loved teasing me when I first fell for Pierre, saying how enamored and found in love I was all the time. Found in love, mama assured, was the only way to be. Together, no matter the direction, if you're with the one that is for you, lost you will never be. My sister was close to being found in love. Joshua was all she could think about.

I was there to open the door when Joshua arrived to pick Sade up for their first date. I had only imagined what Joshua looked like through Sade's descriptiveness when she would talk for hours in awe of his presence.

He had recently moved to Miami from Sicily. They met at a fintech conference social hosted by The Harlem Boutique, a signature hotel on South Beach. The Harlem Boutique is known best for its fine cuisine plated by world renowned chef Sergio Lancelot, at Rooftop, one of the best restaurants on South Beach. Rooftop is  named for its stunning location.  The Harlem Boutique suites also offer breathtaking ocean views, and my favorite of the amenities are the phenomenal spa services.

Joshua won Sade's attention after spending hours together, uninterrupted, talking about economics, finance, commercial real estate  and international business. Joshua spoke modestly yet confidently in my sister's presence leaving her feeling vulnerable and open for the first time in years.

Watching Sade blush as she described Mr. Joshua to me was adorable.  I was overjoyed to see the sparkle he brought to her eyes after just one night of intensive conversation. "Vic!" She gushed! "He's a tall, milk chocolate, breath of heaven. His head bald and alluringly sexy, smile sultry and confident, and his wanton eyes demand undivided attention."  Well damn he got it! My sister was hooked.

When I greeted Joshua, instead of the typical hello, I shook his hand and said firmly,  "I am my sister's keeper." Smiling assuredly, I stepped aside slightly, welcoming him into the house. I walked him to the living room and invited him to sit while waiting for Sade.

*Damn sis! His eyes were inviting and quite commanding.* Sade entered the room just as Joshua was about to sit down and he straightened back up immediately.  I remember his words vividly. "Be still my heart, Sade, you are a true vision of elegance, class and grace. Brilliance and beauty, you make everyone stop and pause when you enter a room.  I am so honored to be in your presence. We've been talking for hours on end now for a month and I have waited for this moment like no other in my life.  Thank you for saying yes."

Debonair in every way, Joshua had my sister head over heels in love from that moment on. The two were inseparable. Looking up at the full moon without a star in sight, closing the door behind them, I knew I'd be seeing a lot more of Joshua. I had my own deposition to have him sit for if he planned to get serious with my sister.

Now, since Joshua has been missing my sweet Sade is a little distant, and rightfully so.  She has loved Joshua completely, mind, body and soul since their first date. Sade hasn't shut me out, but she is shutting in. I feel it desperately when we talk. I see it on her face despite her best efforts to smile and be a positive motivating force in my life.

Sade is forever a big sister, with everything she is going through not knowing what has happened to the love of her life, she still manages to find a breath to focus on what's happening in my world. I wish I could do more to ease Sade's concern and emotional pain.

My family fell in love with Joshua because he loved Sade so purely. He was an amazing husband to her. Pierre couldn't wait for them to come over for Saturday night, date night. Not one time can I recall having a date night with Joshua and Sade that wasn't filled with unending laughter and captivating conversation. We all got along so well.

I could have only hoped that Sade would open up and let love in the way she has with Joshua. We don't speak about our deepest hurt and our blackened hearts to others. There is a hatred that lives deep in my soul for the man that took my sister's happiness. Once my father's business associate, killed execution style, for the death he brought to my sister's innocence, and forever our souls' deepest secret.

## *Victoria*

*Memories of a yesterday that I keep buried lay dormant, for only Sade knows how far I'd really go to save her. We vowed to never tell a soul what happened to her once the damage was done. There was no need to make a public service announcement as some sort of victim. Sade had endured his unwanted advances and acts of molestation, groping and touching her whenever my parents weren't paying attention. After threatening to finally tell our father, Theodore, the monster, scared Sade into thinking that he would kill our mother if anyone found out. The next time our parents left town for a business meeting, Theodore took things to the next level. Angry at my sister for even suggesting she'd tell, he wanted to teach her a lesson, brutally raping her and diminishing her spirit.*

*I'll never forget the look on my sister's face when I picked her body up off the bathroom floor the night I walked in and found him banging her head against the wall while fucking her from behind like a dog in heat. Hearing her screams and the agony in their cacophony made my soul freeze. Black. Everything was black. And then, silence. I shot the man in the back of the head and watched my sister fall to the floor. I picked her up in one full motion and drove her home.*

*He never expected me to find them together. I sensed something was terribly wrong with Sade for a while, and I started following her when she'd leave the house. A master lock picker, getting into his home was not a problem for me. He was too busy shouting his filthy demands, to hear his door chime as I opened it. The rest has tormented me for years.*

*I washed Sade for hours, holding her in the shower as her body fell lifeless, shivering. We* never told anyone about that night and rarely spoke about it to each other. Sade kept apologizing to me for being too weak to tell dad what was happening when it started. Theodore, was a trusted colleague of my father and he manipulated my sister at seventeen, stealing her trust in men and life as a whole. Sade's will to make sure I was okay is the one thing that kept her above water emotionally once this nightmare was over.

We never told daddy. We were mature enough to know that telling anyone in that moment, would only cause further heartache for our loved ones. Mommy and daddy didn't need that. Most of all I know my sister was being quiet to protect me. No matter what, I killed a man in cold blood. And I'd do it again, without question. I felt zero remorse. Only rage for not having known sooner what Sade was going through.

Daddy was there for us on that day without even knowing. If it weren't for him, I wouldn't have known how to kill that motherfucker. Sade and I *learned to shoot at an early age. I took more of a liking to it and would go with dad every chance I got to the shooting range. My favorite times were when dad would take me hunting. I was good with a rifle and I loved the masculinity of Betty, dad's nine millimeter.*

"OKAY ALREADY!" I screamed at the asshole honking his horn like a crazy person behind me, snapping me out of my daydream down horror lane. Typical south Florida traffic filled with impatient drivers from all over the world. The light barely turned green before the jerk-face behind me began to lay on his horn.

Alright Vic, let sleeping monsters lie for today. Focus. I kept telling myself, as I crept closer to the restaurant. Breathe. The sky's beautiful hues of bright blue shining through my sunroof, bring me back to center. It's not often that I lose myself in my memories, but it happens. I will always be my sister's keeper.

## Victoria

*Between losing the first love of her life to death, and her innocence being murdered by the predator whose brains I splattered all over pandora's box, there is no question why I always wish to keep it locked. Sade's high school sweetheart supposedly committed suicide the day he was to reveal his college of choice during the commitment signing ceremony.*

*Ashton was a confident sixteen year old with a 5.0 GPA, and he was our high school's star basketball player since gracing the court with his presence his Freshman year. Sade was never into basketball, until Ashton introduced her to the sport during their Anatomy and Physiology study sessions. Their friendship blossomed and their love was born.*

*My sister has always believed that Ashton was murdered for not choosing the college his coach wanted him to sign with. There had been noticeable tension between the two, but coaches and players go head to head more often than not. There was no reason that I was aware of, to think the coach or anyone in Ashton's camp would want him dead.*

*And then Theodore! I don't like to address the memories that creep into the dark corners of my mind in the middle of the night. I can still hear the gun firing, echoing in my eardrum repeatedly at any given moment. As the years kept passing, I became a better actress, hiding the aftershock from everyone I love. Knowing if I were ever placed in such a predicament again, I would pull the trigger without question. And I would watch as his despicable soul fell to the floor. I am a murderer and I forgave myself for pulling the trigger, but I still struggle to forgive myself when it comes to not knowing sooner that Sade was suffering.*

Here I go again. Snap out of it, I plead with myself necessarily. I hear my voice echo as I catch a glimpse of my eyes. I will the tear drops to hold fast. Now is not the time for all this reminiscing.

We are here, we are strong and this is my moment to take Artistry to the next level.  Focus Victoria.

# Chapter Three - The Board Meeting

After several deep breaths I snap out of it and refocus, regaining control of my thoughts. My girl looks beautiful today. "Good afternoon Cher. " "A gorgeous day it is, hello Vic how are you feeling today?" "I am well Cher, thank you for asking. Early as usual, to make sure all final details are squared away before my first guest arrives." "You know I know you Vic, prepared and always ready before time. Let's catch up after the meeting, we haven't had brunch in a while and we are long overdue." "That sounds great Cher, we'll chat after my board meeting."

Cher is an exotic beauty with lovely jet black curly locks that cascade past the small of her back. Her skin always wore the perfect tan. As hard as Cher worked, she too lived in the sun. Cher is a little lighter than I am and an inch shorter. She's always rocking her heels, so eye to eye is usually how we flow. Her smile is one that lights up the soul and her heart is one of the purest I've been blessed to know. When she 'smizes' her green eyes become the life of the party!

Cher and I became friends about ten years ago. A culinary genius, she is finally leaving her current position as head chef at Capital Grille to open her own restaurant and lounge. I am so very proud of her accomplishments and how driven and focused she's been, working tirelessly to reach her dreams. Her spirit is so motivating. Having grown up in the foster care system, her goal has always been to be able to take care of herself, by herself, while doing something she's passionate about.

We met at Morton's Steakhouse in Fort Lauderdale attending what was for both of us, our first book club meeting. We hit it off immediately and had a blast hanging out together. Joining the book club was a fun way to meet people and enjoy new experiences. Every fourth Friday of the month we would meet for dinner and drinks. Each month we would taste a new Whiskey or Bourbon and discuss our latest book. I was very active in the book club until it dwindled out. Cher and I talked six months ago about rekindling the book club ourselves. One of these days we will get it started again. In the meantime Cher meets me for brunch at least once a month, and we catch up on each other's lives. We skipped last month so it is time for a girl talk session.

Keeping consistent, all of the board members expected in attendance for today's meeting are present and mingling thirty minutes early. It pays to be prepared. I already had copies of the proposal placed before each seat, and the video is set to start. We will start our meeting on time.

"Welcome to our quarterly board meeting. Good afternoon and thank you in advance for your time and attention. I am excited to finally roll out the details for Artistry's latest expansion. We will be starting an entrepreneurship mentoring program. The concept is to have seasoned professionals meet with mentees that have an interest in their respective fields to enhance our members' professional growth potential. Thus far twenty-five entrepreneurs from differing professional backgrounds have agreed to volunteer a set number of hours a week. What I am most excited about is the new scholarship program I have set in place. After hosting my second annual Keep Rising Gala and Concert, I decided the proceeds should roll over into the new scholarship fund program. It gives the gala new vibrancy and meaning. After raising one-hundred thousand dollars the first year and two-hundred twenty-five thousand the second year, I am confident that the next one will exceed my desire to try to double what we've previously raised. The scholarship funds will be rewarded to high school graduates and college students that participate in our programs and meet the necessary requirements."

Everyone seemed genuinely excited thus far. My heart is smiling receiving the supportive energy in the room. I continue. "Art expo will now be twice a month instead of once. We are the hosts for the next six months. As a part of our marketing campaign to let the community know of our newest opportunities, I wanted to draw them to us so more people become comfortable and invested in what we have to offer. It's a great networking opportunity and excellent way to intrigue new business."

The board was excited about the changes. I could have never imagined I'd have two hundred twenty-five thousand dollars in scholarship funds already but I do. Crying with joy inside after receiving board approval, I smiled and adjourned the meeting. "As a reminder, the meeting minutes will be distributed within forty-eight hours of today's meeting. Let's enjoy lunch and toast to growth and expansion."

I sent Cher a text to let her know our meeting was finished. I am looking forward to some one on one time with her after I pack up. Cher peeked her head in the room. "Hey Vic, I'm just wrapping up a few things here. Do you want to meet me at my place in about thirty minutes?" "Sure that sounds great, you know I love your deck, a little piece of heaven while I talk your ear off. How could I say no?" We both giggled. "Great, if I am not there when you arrive just use your key. The Whiskey is on the counter waiting for you. Make sure you use the new monogrammed whiskey glasses I bought. They are on the counter right next to the bar. There is one with your name on it. I will be giving the rest to the girls when we all get together again. Make yourself at home. If you want to take a swim with me, because that is what I intend to do after our toast, feel free to pick one of the new swimsuits out of the guest room closet. I will be relaxing the rest of the day! Smooches, Vic, I'll see you soon." "Yes to all of that. I will see you shortly Cher. Do you need my help here with anything before I head out?" Cher responded before I could finish offering to help. "No, just be ready to celebrate change!"

As I was walking to my car I noticed Daniel, one of the board members holding his head as if he wished to breakdown, yet was doing everything to hold his emotions together. "Hi Daniel, how are you? You seem stressed or upset about something. Is there anything I can do to help?" "I wish," Daniel spoke humbly. "Daniel, I can listen. If you need me, I am here. You are always supportive of me, the business and my family. We are here for you if you need us." "Thank you Victoria, you know I appreciate you. It's just my mother. Since her diagnosis it has been very overwhelming for me. I am trying to be strong twenty-four hours a day, and well, I didn't quite make it today." I understood how Daniel was feeling on so many levels, but for different reasons. Some days can be harder to remain strong than others.

"Daniel, you just learned that your mother is terminally ill. All you can do is be there for her to make her final days as comfortable as possible. It was her choice not to tell anyone she was sick and refuse cancer treatment. You cannot own that burden. Focus on your love for each other and cherish all the time you have left. Forget all the regret and live in the moment. I know it's hard, but you're a devoted son and she knows you love her. Why don't you bring your mother by the house soon and we can have lunch and let her relax by the pool. Pierre can grill and we can enjoy the day watching football and laughing at old times."

A smile began to brighten Daniels saddened face as he responded. "I look forward to it Victoria, I need the release. Thank you, tell Pierre I will be calling him this weekend and we can plan something. Mom will be excited to see you both." "Awesome, sounds great, I'll have my mother, Sade and the twins come over too so your mom can see everyone and finally meet Leo and Lea. My mom is here for the year now. She will be staying to help Sade with the twins so she too will be happy to spend a little time with your mom. Daniel, we love you." I reminded him again blowing a kiss as I hurried to the car.

# Chapter Four - Cher's Chateau

When I arrived Cher wasn't home yet. She sent me a text a few minutes ago saying she would be home in fifteen minutes. I let myself in and went straight to the bar. I poured a glass of whiskey and changed. Pierre called just before my board meeting to let me know that he moved our reservations to nine o'clock tonight, so that gives me a little more time to enjoy girl time with Cher.

Cher's home on Beachfront Avenue is the epitome of serenity. Her back deck offers full view of the Atlantic and is so perfect for entertaining.

Cher inherited twenty-five million dollars from her paternal grandfather. Although she had never met him, he always knew who and where she was. Unable to raise her or be considered for custody, he wrote her a letter with his last will and testament and explained why he had to keep his distance. He asked for her forgiveness, and left her his entire estate.

Although I am still working to gain the emotional strength to be a forgiving being, I do believe that forgiveness is about you. Forgive yourself for what you've done to yourself and/or allowed others to do to you; whether by force or free will, seek to forgive. When forgiveness reigns in your heart, true healing can start. Forgiveness is not defined as forgetting, yet has the power to change the reaction to memories.

Cher had a lot to wrap her mind around without the opportunity to speak to her grandfather and hear the millions of questions swirling in her psyche answered first hand.  He left her an estate which included this beautiful home and a stunning yacht. He also left in trust an additional fifteen million dollars to be divided amongst her immediate heirs if and when she has children.

The sun is so unforgiving today, exactly how I like it. I plugged my phone into the speakers and let Bruno Mars serenade me as I lay poolside sipping whiskey.  "Hey sexy, I'll be right out.  Let me change and grab my glass."  Cher's voice was music to my ears. I'm so happy she's finally home.  I jumped up to speed up the process of toasting with my girl. "I will take care of your glass, you just change, because it is time to toast to your greatness."

I poured Cher's whiskey and dove in for a swim. After ten laps I got out and Cher was walking out of the house looking refreshed and ready to relax. "Today is about celebrating change and growth! And before I forget, Happy Anniversary!" "Thank you, the old married couple has made it another year. I just wish my sister wasn't going through such hell right now." "I know Vic, how is Sade doing with Joshua still missing? Has anyone heard from him? This whole thing just seems so weird to me."

I take in a deep breath and sip my whiskey staring blankly at Cher for a minute considering my words. "Sade is handling life as best she can. She is being very positive. I honestly don't think she will allow herself to think anything other than the fact that Joshua could walk through the door at any moment. I am concerned for her mental state as time continues to pass. I want her to be able to come to grips with the fact that he may never come

seven, and always will be no matter what happens."

Whew, I need another drink. Breathing in deeply, calming my nerves, I exhale and take a sip. "I hear you loud and clear Vic, just know that I am here for you, whatever and whenever you need me, never forget." Lifting our glasses simultaneously, we winked at one another assuredly. "I know sis, I know, I love you Cher." Three whiskey shots later we were all smiles and giggles.

Tonight is going to be beautiful, the weather is perfect. "What are you wearing for tonight's festivities? Get dressed here since Pierre is getting off late, he can come here and you can just have the driver pick up the happy couple from my house. I can help you get all glammed up for the evening. It will be fun!" "Cher, your too good to me!" Just thinking about being pampered by one of my favorite people has me feeling like a queen.

A few more shots in and a plate of delicious berries has me more relaxed than I've been in weeks. "Cher, Is the hot tub on?" "Yes, I turned it on when I got home. You want to hop in?" I know that last question was rhetorical. "Of course, Cher. It's so soothing. Let it soak the stress away. Take my glass with yours, I'll run inside and grab our bottle."

The jets began working their magic. "I had an unexpected visitor last month, Sebastian stopped by." Cher blurted it out as if the words were about to explode inside of her soul if not released immediately. Her heart racing uncontrollably, I grabbed her hand and held it. "Sebastian?" I questioned practically choking on my drink. "When is the last time you heard from him, prior to this visit you're speaking of? Where was Matthew when he stopped by."

Cher's tone softened as she began to explain. "Well, he didn't just stop by, I had noticed a strange vehicle parked just up the block for a couple weeks in the evenings when I would arrive home from work. I've been so overwhelmed with the new restaurant and finishing my tenure at Capital Grill that I just didn't give it much thought. Hindsight is twenty-twenty and of course the moment he banged on my door like someone was attacking him, I knew. All my thoughts rushed to the first day I drove past his car sitting on the side of the road. It wasn't the last car I recall him driving. When we dated he drove a red five series BMW, but this car was a black Lincoln. Sleek and sophisticated, just how he liked his cars."

Staring into Cher's eyes, I had a thousand questions. As if she could hear them burning on the tip of my tongue, she continued. "I didn't let him in at first. It was storming the day he came by and my garage was up. I went out to pull the car in and as I was getting out of the car, I let the garage door down. As soon as I walked back in the house I heard someone banging on the front door. Startled, I froze for a moment then went to the door to see who was there. I didn't see anyone so I stepped away and took a deep breath. Then it happened again and this time I opened the front curtain and peered out. Our eyes met immediately. I saw the black Lincoln in the driveway and knew instantly that he had been watching me and my house for at least two weeks."

I know Cher could read the concern written across my face. My thoughts were racing. "Girl you are scaring me! What did he want and why has he been stalking you. It's weird! Your relationship ended two years ago. When will he finally let go?" I don't want him anywhere near Cher. He was never good for her and she deserves to be free of him completely. "I don't know if he ever will, Cher mumbled."

## Victoria

*Sebastian was the love of her life for five years. Finally she outgrew his abusive ways and left him. Emotionally abusive, Sebastian would constantly talk down to Cher and manipulate her decisions to feed his ego. She lost two restaurant deals prior to this one thanks to his cowardly antics. Cher has been doing so well, getting her life back in order, focusing on herself personally and professionally; and she finally met an amazing man that loves her exactly as she is. Matthew is captivated by her drive and unconditionally supportive of her entrepreneurial dreams. He loves her in a way no one else has, and he's proven time and time again that he can withstand the quicksand of life, remaining by her side through it all. Matthew is everything she deserves in a life partner. I hope someday to be toasting to their nuptials.*

"Cher, I can't believe I am just hearing about all of this." Touching my hand gently, she continued as water welled in her eyes. "For ten minutes I just sat there watching and listening to his sounds and moans. Then finally I asked, why are you here? He held his head up, stood abruptly and began to walk back towards the front of the house. I stood quickly and asked again, he turned and looked me in my eyes and apologized for not loving himself enough to know how to love another properly. I looked at him and asked, why now? He wouldn't speak, staring at the bruises he must have visibly seen on my heart, left from the violent rapture of his words.

Memories that never fade. Why now, Sebastian? I asked again with desperation in my vibrato. He lifted his eyes to mine once more and said that now was all the time he had. I froze and watched him walk away. Victoria, it was the most mind-fracturing experience. I began to obsess about what he meant, and then I realized it didn't matter what he meant. His apologies, or lack thereof are not closure pieces for me. Closure came for me when I decided to require better for myself." I know it hurt, but I could feel the sincerity in Cher's final understanding of closure in this situation.

I know I should close my mouth. I am in shock. Knowing I hold nothing back, Cher was ready for my questions. "Do you think he is dying literally? Has he been sick? Is this like one of those Alcoholics Anonymous twelve-step situations where you make amends for your transgressions? I am in awe that he would have the nerve to just show up here without warning, lay that weird apology on you and walk off. Well, I am glad he walked off, but you know what I mean." Cher let out a nervous laugh and took a sip. "Yes my Victoria, I know exactly what you mean."

"I didn't call you or anyone for that matter. I told Matthew what happened as soon as he got home from his mom's house. Matthew was upset that I didn't text or call while Sebastian was here, but he was understanding. He knew I was in shock. We sat down and I told him every detail of the encounter. Matthew put his feelings aside for that night and held me as I lay awake in silence. The next morning we talked about Matthews feelings and I promised him if it ever happened again no matter where I am, I will call him."

Matthew is the best man that has come into Cher's life. He loves her wholeheartedly without condition, and I love his understanding, yet protective nature.

"Matthew is a good person and loves you genuinely, Cher. I am so glad he was here for you through this." "I am too sis, I couldn't have handled what was to come without him. Four days later we received a package by courier. It was a letter from Sebastian addressed to me and Matthew. In the letter he basically begs Matthew to treat me with the upmost respect and to cherish me for a lifetime. He apologized again to me for not living up to be the man I deserved, specifically for not getting help with his temper and the emotional abuse he delivered effortlessly. I memorized the end of his letter." I listened as Cher recited it as if she'd written the words herself.

### *Sebastian*

*If you are reading this, then I am no longer alive. Cancer has spoken for my life. My spirit is at rest, and I pray you live the life you so very much deserve. Cher, I have included you in my last will and testament. It is the only way I could feel as if I was giving you at least a little bit of what I caused you to lose while with me. I have transferred full ownership of the liquor license to you and I have left you my land in Louisville, Kentucky. The land is yours free and clear. No one in my family has an ounce of claim to it. With the land, you will be able to plan for your ultimate dream of opening your very own distillery. There is a safety deposit box at First Union Bank downtown branch. The information is enclosed. To help you begin building your dream I am leaving twenty million dollars in trust to be used solely for the purpose of this project. Of course the attorneys will explain the details. Matthew, I am humbled to see how a real man supports, loves and protects his woman. May you always be Cher's provider and protector, and Cher, may you never settle for less! Live well, - Sebastian*

"Cher! How could you keep this bottled up inside?" I pulled her close, we nestled into each other and sat quietly, taking the deepest of breaths, exhaling unselfishly.

Cher began to explain her emotions. "It's been a whirlwind. You know how hard and true my love for Sebastian was. I couldn't just ignore his knock at the door, or pretend our eyes hadn't just locked. I wanted to hear what he had to say. I didn't get in depth understanding as to why he was so emotionally destructive, but I am grateful he wanted to apologize and respect Matthew. If this had happened when we first broke up I probably would have lost it. I am in a happy place now with Matthew and his love is so refreshing. He shows me how easy it is to just be me."

Wow, it took Cancer for Sebastian to realize how emotionally destructive he was. "Thanks for sharing this with me. I know it wasn't easy for you to rehash everything. Trust me, I do. Thank goodness you are stronger now, and you know exactly what you want. You deserve the land and the money and much more. Don't you dare feel guilty in the least, and be appreciative for all of your blessings." Cher mouthed "*thank you*" to me and we let it go for now. Celebrate is the word for today!

"I say it's time for hot showers and some makeover fun." "Not just yet missy," Cher sang as she leapt from the chair and ran back into the house. I saw her checking her phone. Then she glanced up at me and motioned for me to come inside. When I did, the doorbell rang, she asked me to answer it as she ran to the restroom. When I opened the door, Sade and Rae surprised me screaming in unison. "Hey!"

I stood there for a second confused with a huge grin on my face and then Cher walked up behind me laughing and clapping. "Come in my loves. I have been waiting for you ladies to arrive." Cher was practically singing. "You know it's hard keeping Victoria in the dark. Let's all sit by the pool so we can tell Victoria about her actual anniversary date. Come ladies walk with me."

Rae walked in sauntering with that I got you look plastered on her face. Her short reddish brown curls bouncing off the nape of her neck with each step. Rae  loves to surprise her friends.  Her hazelnut complexion is glowing as usual. Blowing air kisses with her hazel eyes dancing around the room screaming, *I know something you don't know,* with every blink.  Rae is the tallest of the ladies at 6'.0" without heels she is also the fiercest, most fabulous and beautiful chemist I have ever seen. Her physique stunning and well earned. Rae is dedicated to her workouts and  she believes in keeping negative energy far from her space.

Like most of us, Rae has triggers. She manages hers by keeping her mind, body and thoughts as clean as possible.  All is well in the world, as long as no one bothers the people she loves.  Rae and Cher both have taught me that love is a choice and blood does not determine who one can love. They are forever my sisters from another mother.

We walked over to the dock where Cher's yacht was parked and she pointed. "Tonight, my dear, Pierre has reserved the yacht for just the two of you. You will have a chef on board and a waiter to assist with your needs. The captain has promised smooth sailing. You don't get sneak peaks on the yacht before Pierre arrives. You won't be needing a car, *everyone giggled*, you just need to be ready to ride the waves tonight."

My face, completely blushed pink in awe as my sister, my sweet Sade, begins speaking. Cupping my face, Sade spoke with such endearment. "Little sis, Pierre also sent Rae one thousand dollars as a donation of his appreciation and love for her friendship with you, and all he asked was that she be your personal makeup consultant for the evening."

Turning to face them as their eyes danced with glee, Rae chimed in. "Sade, Cher and I will have you feeling like a queen this evening. Brace yourself, he also gave Sade his credit card to purchase five dresses she thought you would love for the evening with accessories to match for each. All you have to do is choose one and then we will return any that you don't want to keep in your wardrobe."

I began to cry tears of happiness. Looking from Rae to Cher and then seeing the peace in my sister's eyes, Sade was smiling, and that made me so happy. In this moment, if only for this moment, she was happy. If not for herself, then at least for me. Just being alone with Pierre is always enough romance for me, and when he goes and plans elaborate dates just to remind me how much he loves me, my heart melts like a school girl experiencing her first kiss. The purity and innocence that rests with overwhelming excitement showers me.

Sade, Cher and Rae are beautiful blessings in my life. Words can never truly express how much love I have for these ladies, my sister's for life. "This calls for a toast! Here's to my favorite girls, thank you for loving me exactly as I am. Thank you for your constructive criticism and praise through the years. We have grown in love and life together, with still so much more life to live. I am grateful to call you family, and I can't wait to be pampered! Just don't forget, since we are all here together, let it be known that the next girls evening will be for us all to be pampered and celebrate each other. I love you all so very much."

# Chapter Five - It's Our Anniversary

Sometimes I wonder what I did right to deserve such an amazing husband and life partner in Pierre. I am blessed. He is so attentive and sensitive to my needs, while remaining decisive, confident and always protecting my best interest. "Ladies, I am so thankful to you all for being here with me this evening to help me celebrate my anniversary. I haven't had this much fun in a very long time. I needed it, and I needed all of you. Group hug!" We all smiled and brought it in. My sweet Sade whispered, "I love you little sis," while holding on to our hug for dear life.

Sade cleared her throat and then proceeded to open the closet. We were in what I liked to call Vic's guest room, of course that just means it's my favorite room in Cher's house and where I sleep whenever we have our girls nights in. I've had an amazing, hot shower, and now I am ready to decide on my dress for the evening. As soon as I saw them I cried. The girls had no idea why, except for Sade of course, so she was the only one standing there unconcerned about my tears.

Rae couldn't take it anymore, she had to ask. "What the hell are you crying for woman?" And like magic, I started laughing through the tears, but the words wouldn't come out fast enough for Rae. "Hello! One minute you're in tears and the next your laughing hysterically. Someone clue us in please!"

Sade and I were both laughing at this point and she knew which dress I would choose. Rae shouted again, "Hello!"

"Okay Sade, I better tell Rae and Cher what's up before Rae jumps us all." Smiling slyly, I continued. "Apparently my sister and my husband have acquired the latest sketches that I have been working on tirelessly to complete for Fredricka. Well, they are finished and I don't know how but what I have before me is art in motion. These two beautiful souls have found a seamstress to bring one of my masterpieces to life. I know Sade picked out this particular sketch because I told her when I originally showed them to her which was my favorite.

And now, here before me with my closest friends, I get to wear my own design tonight. I truly feel like royalty ladies, you have no idea! I never could have imagined this. I hope Pierre loves it."

Rae and Cher locked eyes in shock and simultaneously sighed in awe. "That is the most romantic part of this evening and you haven't even stepped foot on the yacht yet. The thought of Pierre going through all that trouble to find someone to make your masterpiece come to life as an anniversary present is such a beautiful gesture." Rae sang his praises while setting up the vanity for glam makeover fun.

"Obviously I am choosing to wear my own dress tonight. I couldn't fathom wearing someone else's designs after what my man pulled off for me. I just pray he likes what he sees!" My heart was fluttering with excitement. "Girl! He will more than like what he sees!" Rae was always unapologetically honest and full of sass. She smiled and gave me her once over side eye and said, "Park it in the chair missy." And park I did. With Rae's makeovers you are not permitted to look in the mirror or see yourself until her work is completely finished.

As I sit here being pampered sipping whiskey neat with my favorite ladies, excitement completely overwhelms me. Tonight will be the first time I will be wearing one of my very own designs.

Sade could tell I was getting a little nervous so she put MJB's My Life album on and the singing soothed my heart. Cher and Sade started dancing around the room like they were making their own music video. Forty minutes later, my face had been transformed, as Rae would say. I looked in the mirror and I felt like the most beautiful girl in the world. "Rae, I love it. Thank you so much!" "You're welcome my lovely." We air kissed and joined in the fun, dancing and singing.

The phone ringing startled us out of our dancing and singing high. Cher answered the phone abruptly, trying to slow her breaths.

Immediately her facial expression changed. Sade asked, "Why does Cher look like you after pulling the trigger in my nightmare?" Lost in her expression, I knew exactly what my sister meant.

Rae lowered the music and Sade and I sat on the bed staring at Cher. We couldn't figure out who was on the other end and Cher was barely saying anything on her end. Making non-verbal gestures and soft sounds of agreement, she looked at us and tried to smile, but the corners of her mouth remained stagnant. As she leaned in to hang up the phone, we all shouted in unison. "What's wrong Cher?"

Cher just stood still for about five minutes, frozen. Of course it seemed like an hour before she moved a muscle. Cher looked at me and broke down. She fell to the floor as her body went limp. I knelt before her and spoke in a hushed tone. "Who was on the phone?" She looked up at me and said, "Joshua." "JOSHUA!" We all yelled, feeling the fire boiling in my soul, I stood up, looked at Sade, and blurted out question after question.

"Why would Joshua be calling here after all this time?" Not leaving time for an answer I turned to

Cher and continued. "What did he say?  How did he know we were here?  Did he ask for Sade? Hello!"

I can't, my breaths quickened as I looked over seeing my sister's eyes welling up. I knew it was a matter of time before every bottled up emotion she's hidden in concern for her husband would be let loose. The flood gates of her heart are now flowing freely, she can't speak.

Cher stood up slowly, Rae at her side, in shock, helping her up. Rae held her for a minute before speaking.  "Cher, you have to find the words to express what just happened."  Through gasping breaths, Cher spoke.  "It wasn't Joshua, it was someone claiming to know who and where he was. The person said that if we ever wanted to see Joshua alive again, we would need to pay a five million dollar ransom."  Cher was in a state of shock and rightfully so.

Anger was flowing through my veins like the raging waters of the Nile.  I stared into my sweet Sade's eyes and dove into protection mode. *I am Victoria, and I am my sister's keeper.*

"What the fuck do you mean ransom?" Who the hell would want to kidnap Joshua? Sade, baby do you have any idea why or who would want to do this to your family? Does Joshua have any enemies that you are aware of?"

Sade finally uttered a sound. "Cher," was all she could get out before going silent again. Cher walked over, sat with her and spoke calmly. "I don't know how they know my number or knew that you would be here, but I am so glad we are all here with you right now. This is not news we would want you to hear while alone. This could be a good thing. Asking for ransom means most likely Joshua is still alive." Cher tried to speak with assurance through the trembles she could not shake away.

With so many questions and zero answers all I could think to do was call Pierre. The day, afternoon and evening were going so perfectly until a few minutes ago. Pierre didn't answer so I sent him a text asking him to call me ASAP! I am hoping he will respond immediately. I pray he doesn't think I'm just trying to find out information about all the anniversary surprises he's planned.

I turned to look at my aquamarine dress hanging on the outside of the closet door awaiting its first night out. For a quick second a smile crossed my face, seeing my art in motion hanging before me. Wow! There's no way I can enjoy the rest of the evening now. I can't leave Sade's side. I won't.

I don't know much about Joshua's business dealings other than to understand that he has done extremely well for himself in commercial real estate. I need to call my investigator and let him know what's happening here.

Cher came running back into the room with the house phone ringing in her hand screaming, "It's Pierre!" I snatched the phone from Cher's grip.

"Hello." "Hi my Victoria, are you getting ready for our anniversary fun. I can't wait to see you, we've got amazing plans this evening, and I hope you like all of your surprises thus far." I love this man with all that is within me.

"Yes Pierre, I was speechless when Sade pulled the dresses out. I love you so very much, but that's not why I called. Babe, I don't think we can celebrate tonight. I won't be able to get Joshua off of my mind." "Joshua?" Pierre's voice was filled with confusion. "What's happening, did he call Sade? Is he home? Victoria, what is going on?" I could hear his voice begin to tremble as his last words were octaves higher than when he first said hello.

Pierre is extremely protective of me and everyone I love, so of course he would be ready to move mountains for my sweet Sade whenever necessary. "Pierre, in the middle of being pampered by my girls, Cher received a phone call. The woman on the other end threatened her saying that if she didn't receive five million dollars ransom, we would never see Joshua alive again. We can't understand why they called Cher, or how the woman knew we all would be here." "Woman?" Pierre's voice pierced through the phone. "Yes, a woman made the ransom call. She said she would be calling back again tomorrow with details for exchanging the money." "Did you call the police?" "No Pierre, I could only think to call you. I also need to call Javier, to let him know about the ransom call." "I'm on my way there Vic, I'll see all of you in fifteen minutes, put me on speaker phone please." "Okay babe, hold on."

Pierre cleared the pool of emotions swirling through his mind. "Ladies I am on my way there. Do not open the door for anyone you don't know and please remind Vic to call Javier as soon as I hang up. Cher, I am so sorry that all of this is going on at your home, but I am so grateful you are all together. Rae, my sparring partner, hold it down for me till I get there!" Rae giggled, "I got you big brother." Sade broke the silence of her thoughts. "Pierre, please hurry." My sister's voice was lowered to a whisper as if she was taking her final breath. Pierre understood. "Vic, you are my world and I love you. I am on my way, take care of each other." After hanging up the phone my girls and I just held each other in silence for a moment.

What had Joshua gotten himself into? Ransom? Five million dollars? My head was spinning. I looked over at Rae as she returned the glance, I let out a lasting sigh. "My sweet Sade, what's going through your mind right now sis?"

Sade looked at me and tried to express herself through sobs. "I don't understand any of this. I have been through his things. I didn't find anything that would indicate he was in trouble or had been dealing with any individuals that would want to hurt him. I don't get involved in his business dealings. He hasn't mentioned any issues to me, but with the pregnancy and the twins I don't think he would want to alarm me with details. He's so protective of me, always. He didn't even talk to Pierre about it. I mean usually he will confide in Pierre when he's stressed and needs perspective, but nothing was said. Does Javier know anything? And when did you decide to involve Javier exactly? You never mentioned it to me."

Grabbing both of my sister's hands, I squeeze and pull her in close. Speaking with sincere strength, I repeated continuously, "I am my sister's keeper." Our eyes locked in a gaze; Sade nodded in understanding. Rae and Cher surrounded us and together we are bonded. Holding my shoulders firm, Rae clears her throat. "I have you both, now and always. I got you!" Cher smiled at Rae and confirmed, "Yes, we got you."

I just sent Javier a text to call me ASAP regarding Joshua. I am sure he will call shortly. He's usually really good at getting back to me quickly.

"Vic, what am I supposed to do? My children? My family? I need my husband home! I don't care about the money, I just want him back and I need answers!" With each statement Sade's voice trembled more. Her sadness was turning to anger, and pain was written all over her face. "I know Sade, I know. We will get through this together."

My sister's eyes wept of worry and abandonment. The reddish-pink stains on the white of her eyes are glossed over with misgiven trust and unreturned loyalty. Looking down as if to see hundreds of feet beneath her feet, Sade's voice began to crack as she let sadness speak. "I'm so sorry for ruining your anniversary plans. I was having so much fun celebrating you and being here with our girls. It was a nice break for me and now this. What did I do to deserve this? Why is this woman trying to tear my family apart? Who does she work for?"

Through all of this my big sister still feels the need to apologize to me. "Sade none of this is your fault. You haven't ruined anything for me. Right now, you are my number one priority. Pierre would have it no other way, and you know that!"

"You got that right!" Rae chimed in, stepping back into the room. "This shit is not your fault Sade. Let's stop that thought process now. I had to give my love, Stephen a call to let him know what was going on. My rock, you already know, he's ready to come through the phone to be here. He sends his love and said he will be flying back into town tomorrow."

I love the way Stephen treats Rae, he loves her dearly. I hope their relationship lasts a lifetime. They are perfect for each other. Fighting back the tears, I held Rae's hand, and no words were needed. We both needed to hit the punching bag something serious.

We all need to band together to figure this out and protect Sade. Cher walked back into the room and told us all to come to the living-room. She had the phone to her ear, she was talking to Matthew. As we were walking back into the living-room, the doorbell rang and we all damn near jumped out of our skin. Cher hung up the phone, turned to fill us in. "Matthew is on his way. Rae, get the door, it's probably Pierre."

# Chapter Six - Anticipation

Rae let out a sigh and stood to walk towards the door. The rest of us slowly turned our bodies staring at the door as if the grim reaper was on the other side. The piercing sound rang in our ears again as Rae peeped through the curtain. "It's Pierre." She opened the door and he stood there with arms wide open. "Bring it in sparring partner," my love said, hugging Rae tightly. "How are the rest of the ladies holding up?" Rae gave him the side eye and a smile before responding. "You know we got each other, but this shit is crazy, Pierre."

Pierre stood in silence for what seemed like an eternity, his arms wrapped around every inch of my body. Whispering "I love you," I leaned back and our eyes locked. We both knew tonight was no longer about us. I buried my head back into his chest resting in each heartbeat. And then it happened again, the phone rang. This time Pierre answered the phone. "Hey man, yes I'm here. Don't worry you know I'm not going anywhere. I'll let Cher know you will be here in a few." We all took a deep breath and sat down. We knew it was Matthew on the other end of the call. Although Matthew had just spoken to Cher, he had to call back again to check on things. I know there was relief in his soul when he responded to Pierre answering his house phone. Brothers, Pierre understood wholeheartedly.

My sister is everything to me. I have to help her get through this. My eyes now a bloodshot hue of anger mixed with confusion. I am my sister's keeper. To the depths of the Mariana Trench, there is no limit to how deep I will dive to keep my sweet Sade safe. Windchimes pierce my thoughts and my anxiety is revved up. "Grab my phone Rae, it might be Javier texting me back." The windchimes sounded again, announcing a text message. She grabbed the phone. It was Javier; Rae read his message aloud.

> *I traced the number for you and I prefer to share the details in person. Ask Cher if I can come there to speak with everyone while*

*Sade has the support she will undoubtedly need...*

Of course his discreteness and urgency permeated through all of our bodies. Rae quickly sent him a text back for me.

*YES! YES! YES! We are here waiting. See you shortly. Thank you Javier.*

Pierre got up and walked over to Sade. He put his hand on her shoulder and her body went limp. She hurled over shaking and rocking her body back and forth. Glimpsing up at Pierre, her eyes asking why, without words being spoken.

Pierre responded instantly, holding Sade close, as if he understood the question unspoken. "I don't know Sade, but I trust Joshua and I believe he would come back to you if he could. I don't have the answers, but you and my niece and nephew are safe. I have taken it upon myself to move you and the twins into our house for a few weeks. I did not ask your sister, I sought your mother's assistance. This is my idea and what I need to do for peace of mind. This is not up for debate. I love you as my own sister, and I refuse to let anything happen to you now that I know you have been threatened. Mom will be with us temporarily also." I leaned in, placing my hand on the small of Pierre's back. I loved the way he loved me and my family so purely. Pierre continued. "I have hired twenty-four hour private security for both houses as additional protection, especially with no one living on the property right now. Once Javier arrives and we hear what he has to say, then we will plan our next steps."

There was a loud bang, and Pierre stood up immediately. Cher ran to the garage door and flung it open. As Matthew stepped into the doorway, Cher leapt into his arms, her legs wrapped around his waist, arms holding on for dear life and her head planted in his neck. He peeped his head up slightly to greet us, his voice filled with compassion. "I'm so pissed I wasn't here for all of you." Cher still holding on, softly interrupted. "I'm so happy you're home. It's been a nightmare without you." Gently laying Cher down on the chaise, he leaned in and kissed her forehead, then sat next to Sade. Speaking to Sade as if she were his own sister, with such the perfect mix of tenderness and protectiveness, Matthew said, "We got you." His words send a flood of warmth through my soul.

Lightly placing his hand on her shoulder, Matthew looked at Rae and asked her to go to his office and make sure the security camera screens were all on and showing properly. Then Mathew gave Pierre the nod, and they walked outside alone and sat by the pool to talk. Brothers from another mother, it's a blessing that our husbands and significant others are as close as they are. We are family by choice, in love and life.

I was looking for Rae and she was nowhere to be found. Cher was making tea for Sade and all I wanted was a Louisville Whiskey Margarita and Cuban Cigar. I needed Rae for that. Time to sip and breathe. I heard a clinking sound and then it dawned on me. Rae had slipped into the weight room on the third floor. Those had to be dumbbells I heard clinking.  It was one of the few places that Rae could completely tune out the world and realign her strength. The weight room, boxing gym, sunshine and beaches keep Rae's emotions balanced.

Rae, I called out to her as I made it to the third floor. "Yes sis, I'm in here Vic."  Wrapping her wrists as I walked in I knew what time it was.  Rae hugged the bag for a second looked at me and I knew my job was to hold the bag for my Rae of sunshine.  I held firm and listened.  "You're the only one who can handle holding the bag for me besides Pierre,  and I need to kick ass right now! This bag will have to do." I hear you sis, I got you Rae."  For the next 30 minutes, Rae and I took out our frustrations on the bag until the doorbell rang again.

Cher answered the door.  "Hello Javier, come in. Thank you so much for everything we are eager to hear what you've learned."

Sade was laying on the couch when Javier arrived. Her eyes hazed, she slowly sat up as Javier approached. Javier wiped the tears from Sade's face, embracing her lovingly. His voice was heavy. "Hello my dear." She let his words linger, loud now, in the still of silence.

Matthew and Pierre walked into the living room and we all gathered around. "What's up man?" Pierre said shaking Javier's hand. "Everything and anything my brother." "Where's Rae? Stephen called me this morning, very concerned about her. We know how she can get when she feels the need to protect her loved ones. She is loyal to no end. If Rae loves you, there's nothing she won't do to protect you." "I'm right here Javier." Rae's voice was filled with renewed energy, as she glided down the stairs, unwrapping her wrists.

Cher walked back out of the kitchen with a shot of whiskey for everyone. Placing a glass in each hand, she demanded Javier spill the news. For what seemed like an hour, Javier stood in silence with a blank stare. Then, as I was about to blurt out obscenities, Javier spoke firmly, looking into Sade's eyes. "I traced the number from the ransom call and it is registered to Raymond International, an export/import company. After further research I believe the company is a shell company for Sicilian Arms Dealer Angelo Lea. "Lea!" Sade blurted out without hesitation. "Yes, Lea." Javier confirmed and continued. "During my tenure with the Federal Bureau of Investigation, I spent a lot of time tracking and researching this man. There is also a beautiful mansion on Fisher Island listing Raymond International as the owner, furthering my theory that Raymond International is a shell company. I am looking into international properties owned by Raymond International also to cross reference whether or not Joshua and the company had any legal real estate dealings. I know this doesn't sound like much, but it's a start."

I could see the confusion building to higher heights in my sister's eyes. I kissed her forehead, and turned to Javier. "It is far more than a start Javier, we appreciate having some new information." Javier smiled. "Thank you for that Vic, I appreciate your understanding in a time where patience is the hardest. My personal assistant will call me as soon as any updates cross her desk. In the meantime, Sade, do you have access to Joshua's work files, his client lists and other similar pertinent information associated with his business dealings? There may be some names there that stand out to me from my former dealings undercover."

Pierre responded on her behalf. "Yes, of course, I will meet you at Sade's house to provide you with the access needed." My sweet Sade squeezed my hand tightly as I said thank you again to Javier for all of his efforts.

Rae's cell rang and it was Stephen. Her face lit up immediately. She let out a sigh of relief and ran to the door. Stephen was there waiting eagerly, smiling with the phone in his hand. As she flung the door open he grabbed her by the waist and held on for dear life, kissing her a thousand and one times. Finally she felt relief, to not be quite as strong for a few moments, resting in the arms of her love. Stephen is the only man to stand the test of time and outlive Rae's cemented exterior and embrace her vulnerability. He is her rock, and she is his sunshine.

# Chapter Seven - Bourbon Princess

Stephen entered the house, speaking to everyone, he walked over to Sade, and embraced her. As he held her, the tears just kept flowing. I rubbed her back and Rae went into the kitchen with Cher to get water for everyone. Cher handed Pierre, Javier and I water, and then decided that everyone should stay at her home tonight.

Before anyone could counter her proposal, Cher kept speaking. "Matthew is the only one that knows the new location of the restaurant, but now keeping it a surprise seems irrelevant. I will be the first Sicilian woman to own a restaurant on Fisher Island. The Blessing is that I have paid for the land and own the building outright.

My stare was unbreakable. I had no idea Cher had already accomplished so much entailing the move. "While this is not the time to celebrate that, it is the time to be wise. Due to the restaurant and my dealings on Fisher Island, we can come and go as we need without issue. We can use the Bourbon Princess to travel back and forth. The other surprise is that I have built a stunning home on the land with mother-in-law quarters for your parents when they visit and two guest houses. I have a tennis court, olympic size pool and all the amenities we could hope for. So, surprise family! But for now, Javier, you have full access. We can set you up in one of the guest houses so while you're there you can have a local office. Let my assistant Christina know what you need and she will take care of it."

Listening to Cher tell us about her dream property for one short second brought a smile to my heart. In the midst of such agonizing heartache, in that second, my body wasn't numb. Cher welcomed us into her home without room for objection.

Cher took a breath. In awe, Sade stood, grabbed Cher's hands and held them both tightly in the palm of hers. Whispering softly, Sade said, "Thank you." Looking around at everyone, she thanked us repeatedly. Cher replied assuredly. "We are family, all of us. You know how I feel about family and love based on my existence in this world. Love is a choice. I chose you a long time ago sis and there is absolutely NOTHING you can do about it. Now, understand this, the time for shock, knowing what we are facing, is over! Now we FIGHT! If anyone needs clothes check the red guest room on the second floor. There are new items in there and I am sure there is something for everyone." Taking in a deep sigh, I can tell Cher is fighting back nervousness to be strong for Sade, for us all.

Cher continued speaking before anyone could interrupt. "Also, fresh toiletries and personal items can be found in each guest bathroom. The pool house we all know is fully stocked with swimwear for everyone."

Matthew put his arm around Cher's shoulders and replied in agreeance. "The calm before the storm, tonight we plan and prepare for tomorrow morning we will head to Fisher Island at nine o'clock."

Sade called mom to let her know what was going on. We could hear her cries through the phone. Pierre assured me that mom knew what was happening regarding the move into our home and the heightened security, however it is still overwhelming for her to comprehend. She is rightfully concerned about her daughter, grandchildren and of course her son-in-law.

"I flew your uncle and aunt into town to stay at our house and help your mother with the children. Of course she too will love the company and distraction so she isn't alone when we aren't home." "Thank you Pierre for all that you've done. You are my rock." "You're welcome, I love you Vic."

My mom and her twin brother have always been extremely close. That's why the family was so excited when we found out that Sade and Joshua were having twins.

Taking the phone from Sade, I talked to mom for thirty minutes longer. I assured her that everything would be okay and that we would give her regular updates. She wanted to know why we haven't shared our latest findings with the police. I explained that was actually not the case. "As of tomorrow, the FBI will most likely be involved based on the research Javier has presented. Javier is currently waiting on further information from his assistant and then we will move forward from there. We leave for Fisher Island on Cher's yacht first thing tomorrow morning." "Okay dear, put the speaker phone on." Mom insisted, her voice was crystal clear. "Hello, I love everyone and I am so grateful that you are all in this together supporting one another. You're all my babies, and I need you to have each other's back!" In unison we all screamed, "We love you too mom! Always!"

After receiving the love from mom through the airwaves, a sense of relief washed over me, over all of us. "Well family, I say we take a deep breath, head to the pool house, get changed and board the *Bourbon Princess* since dinner and drinks are already prepared for the evening." Sade and Cher both looked at me and said, "Yes! Vic, let's do it!" Cher grabbed Sade by the arm and said to everyone, "I don't want to think about anything but the hot tub on my yacht, the whiskey in my glass, MJB coming through my speakers and all that great cuisine Pierre had prepared for your anniversary."

Stephen and Matthew headed to the boat first and got everything set up as the girls and I went to change in the pool house. Pierre and Javier motioned to let me know they'd be right out after they finished looking at the information Javier's assistant had just forwarded to his email. I blew him a kiss and kept walking. One thing's for sure, whatever they've just received, I don't want to hear about it until tomorrow morning. Tonight as Matthew said, is the calm before the storm and I intend to bask in it.

Cher surprised us with a tray of her amazing hors d'oeuvres including my favorite, buffalo cauliflower. Remembering the first time I tasted buffalo cauliflower at a gorgeous rooftop bar in Wynwood, has my mouth watering. I will be eating and drinking until my heart's content tonight.

Sade raised her glass with tears streaming down her face ready to toast. "I know you are all here for me ultimately, and I appreciate it. I couldn't have imagined in a million years that I would be experiencing such a nightmare. My life partner, my soulmate, my Joshua, is literally gone and for a while it felt like he disappeared without a trace. I finally feel like hope is rising even with the little answers we've managed to uncover. It scares me at times because I haven't fully broken down." Pausing for a moment Sade inhaled forcibly.

My sister is right, she's cried but she hasn't truly broken down. Sade hasn't allowed herself the vulnerability of unmasking every ounce of her pain. For now its seeping at the seams of her veins relentlessly, waiting to pour out unbiasedly.

Exhaling slowly letting the air seep into existence, my sweet Sade continued and we listened intently. "I keep going as if at any moment Joshua will walk through the door. With each passing day I was feeling weaker until the ransom call. Oddly enough, as heart-wrenching as it was to receive the ransom call, it was something. Now I feel like we have direction. I don't know for the life of me how Joshua could have gotten involved with an arms dealer, but I am hoping that Javier and Pierre can find more information after combing through Joshua's office and work files. I pray you all know how much I love and appreciate your unconditional support." "We got you always big sis, you know this." Sade wiped her tears. "Yes, Vic, I know this." On cue, Rae turned on the deck speakers, and like clockwork Cher was the first to start dancing. She pulled Sade by the hand and the fun began.

Three whiskey fire shots in, Stephen text Rae to let us know to come aboard. At that moment Javier and Pierre walked out with glasses in hand ready to let go for the evening. And just like that, with the push of a button we went from MJB to old school hip hop. Mic in hand, two shot karaoke was about to begin. "Oh that's my jam, *It Takes Two*" ... Pierre came up behind me, placed his hand on the small of my back and started rocking the mic with me.

Once everyone had a couple rounds of karaoke, we moved on to whiskey pong. The ladies always win, but I'm not sure this time, our men are overly amped tonight for obvious reasons. I don't mind losing whiskey pong, but spades is all mine tonight. Rae was always my spades partner and playing against Pierre and Stephen is nonstop humor. We are all so animated it's hilarious. Javier, Sade, Matthew and Cher enjoyed the hot tub while we took these men to school on the spades table. Javier is supposed to teach all of us how to play Texas hold em'. No need to let him know that Sade and I started taking poker lessons a while ago. We wanted a little edge on Mr. competition.

# Chapter Eight - The Morning After

I could hear the waves crashing against the side of the yacht. My eyes still dazed, I opened them slowly welcoming the sunshine and sea breeze. For a split second I felt a moment of relief. Taking in slow breaths, deep cleansing of toxicity, releasing. Still in bed, I turned over to say good morning and I realized that I was alone. Right! What was I thinking? The calm before the storm. Now the eye is in full focus, like a hurricane ready for landfall, seek shelter, because I am coming for what's mine! *About last night ...*

I jumped right up, threw my sundress on and headed to the house. Looks like I'm the last to rise. My body, mind, shit, my everything was drained and tired beyond understanding. I guess that's why I slept like a baby after last night.

Hey fam, good morning. "Your Kentucky bourbon coffee awaits sis," Cher called from the second floor. Okay, let me pour and I'll be right up. The guys were in their own world finalizing the plans for Fisher Island. Rae was in the weight room, at one with the bag, while Cher and Sade were packing so we have what we need for a few days.

When I walked into the weight room to see Rae she was drenched in sweat, beats headphones blaring. I could hear MJB telling the world *"I'm fine, fine, fine!"* There's nothing like a little Mary motivation when you're at one with the punching bag. Yes, we all love the raw realness of MJB, past and present. She is an amazing artist and story teller. She's always in heavy rotation.

I walked to the other side of the bag so I could catch Rae's eye. She looked up and took one side of her headphones off. "Morning sis." Rae winked, leaned over and we air kissed. I asked her if she had spoken with Sade this morning. Rae smirked. "Girl, you know your sister, she is back to beast mode with her emotions placed on the shelf. She was the first one up, and when I walked into the weight room she was waiting for me. Wrists wrapped and gloves ready. I didn't ask her any questions, I knew she was finally ready for her lessons. For 45 minutes she punched her emotions in the face repeatedly until she felt empowered to start the day."

I was curious about her demeanor. We have no idea what we are going to find, and I am certain we haven't even scratched the surface. I have tried to put on a brave face for my sister, but no one has taken the time to mention that Joshua was a Navy Seal prior to becoming a real estate broker. He is a trained killer to be frank. I know we never discuss it as a family, but it's time to stop skirting this reality with my sister. Sade has to have thought about it. Yet, no one has said anything. Pierre and I haven't even said a word about it to each other, however I know he thought about it. He's just been quiet, placing puzzle pieces one by one while keeping the conversations in his head.

"Rae, have you thought about the fact that Joshua was a Navy Seal prior to coming into our lives?" "Now, you already know I was all over it in my head Vic, but I wasn't going to be the first to awaken the *elephant* in the room. To answer your question, yes, it has been on my mind constantly.

Whatever we know is just the tip of the iceberg. I feel it in the depths of my soul Vic. We better get our showers, we need to get out of here shortly."

Rae was right, we needed to get moving. I have to make some phone calls to delegate at work so the event goes off without a hitch while I focus on Sade. Stepping into Matthew's office, I pushed the door leaving it slightly ajar, and immediately my knees buckled. My heart is breaking for my sister and not knowing what's to come is breath catching. The nerves are suffocating at times and I just want to explode. I haven't had migraines in years and they've returned. Keeping quiet is treacherous to the conversations in my heart. Nothing is about me. Everything is about Sade. She needs all of me. Any inclination that my migraines have returned, and she will immediately drop everything, even under the circumstances. Pandora's box of blackouts, one my big sister and I vowed never to let reopen.

## Victoria

*From the moment I pulled the trigger many moons ago, saving my sister from the devil that still haunts my dreams, my life has never been the same. I still have migraines when my stress levels are extremely high. My sleep is non-existent, and when I do sleep, I am plagued with the vivid scenes of Sade's rape. I don't know if I will ever forgive myself for not getting there sooner. I will always feel as if I should have picked up on some clues regarding the type of distress my sister was under. I cry too, still, in the dead of night and I awake to Pierre holding me tight. Sade has only ever shown gratitude for me arriving when I did, and she has begged me to forgive myself. I am not sure that I will ever be able to do that. I am my sister's keeper.*

Snapping out of it, I stood, made the necessary phone calls, took a shower and changed within thirty minutes. Walking out onto the patio I sat next to Cher and Sade. Rae walked out behind me with Javier, Matthew and Stephen.

Pierre commanded our attention as he began to explain our next steps. "Stephen, Rae and Javier will fly there. Stephen will keep the plane in a private air strip that few are aware exists on the island. One of his clients has extended the courtesy under the circumstances. Don't ask too many questions just listen to the details. We have two methods of arrival and departure. Only one, we must not mention. Stephen trusts his client's discretion. A car has already been provided and will be waiting for them at the hanger upon arrival. The keys will be in the glove compartment with a cell phone. Use that phone in case of emergency until we arrive instead of your regular cell phones. And yes, for precautionary reasons I have burner phones for everyone. I need us to go off the grid for a while, at least until answers start unfolding. Don't worry, I have a way to communicate with the family and check on everything at home. We just need to focus."

Pierre fell silent for a moment. He looked into each of our eyes one by one saving Cher for last, holding less urgency in his stare, his heart filled with gratitude.

Cher gave Pierre a nod, snapping him out of his thoughts, Pierre continued. "Cher has made arrangements for the house to be fully stocked with food and any other necessities we may need while there. If anyone asks, we are there with Cher supporting her restaurant opening. Javier can explain further what he's discovered once we all arrive at Cher's on the island. Just know that the elephant in the room has been subdued by the lion in my soul. For anyone who has wondered whether or not I have thought about the fact that Joshua was a former Navy Seal, the answer is yes. What you don't know is why. I will explain that once we arrive at Cher's."

Javier noticed the fear in Sade's eyes, and began speaking to Sade directly. "All of these measures are necessary to ensure our safety, and connectivity while investigating under the radar. I know this is overwhelming to everyone, but trust me, I will do everything I can to keep you all safe and get the answers you seek. Pierre and Vic are like family to me, you all are, and there is nothing I won't do to support you Sade."

Javier froze for a moment, lost in the depths of his thoughts, undoubtedly about his true feelings for my sister.

### *Javier*

*I remember the first time I asked Sade out on a date. It was a beautiful spring day, and I had taken a walk downtown to enjoy a cup of tea at my favorite spot. Sitting in the window, I was in awe of the energy that illuminated her presence when she walked in and ordered a chai tea latte. In all innocence, the first time I saw her, I did not know who she was or that our paths would ever cross again in such a way. I asked her to join me and she agreed. We talked for hours about politics, and the financial destruction of our government. Her intelligence was the most alluring and sexy part of her presence. Although we enjoyed our happenstance tea date, Sade declined to go out again.*

*The next time I saw Sade, was a couple years later at her sister's home. I was invited to Vic and Pierre's house party, and surprise, that's when we both realized that we had met previously. Without dwelling on that, we hugged, and I was introduced to Joshua for the first time that day. I mentioned the prior encounter with Sade to Pierre, the day I showed up for the party. I felt a since of obligation, like he should know that I had met and enjoyed the company of his sister-in-law in the past. He promised to keep it in confidence.*

*Still single, I hope someday she finds the strength to love again, because there is nothing I wouldn't do for a second chance with Sade.*

*Snapping out of my daze, I tried to focus on the information Pierre was telling us. For a moment it was like I was in a tunnel wondering what if. Maybe if I had pursued Sade more years ago, and not taken her first no for an answer, she would have never met Joshua. Maybe. I know I'll never know, but maybe.*

Matthew and Cher locked up everything and Stephen, Rae and Javier left for the airport. My thoughts were consumed with the need for answers. Pierre has been keeping something from me, and I feel like it is going to hit me like ten tons of bricks. I hear his words echoing in my head. *"What you don't know is why."* What is he talking about? Why now?

Docked at Cher's we arrived midmorning with a nice amount of daylight left to set things in motion. I thought about what Pierre said before we left the house. I keep replaying his words over and over in my head and I can't for the life of me think of what he could be keeping from me. Then to top it off, the look Javier was giving Sade while Pierre was explaining everything was lasting. It was as if there was a novel of their history together written in the depths of his eyes.

"I can't take this shit anymore Pierre, let's all sit down and hear what this big damn secret is that you have been holding!" Pierre looked around the room, grabbed me by the arm, pulled me back outside and walked me back towards the yacht, while everyone else stayed inside to settle in.

Pierre called back to them so no one would follow him. "We'll be right back!" Then he turned to me cupping my chin in his hands lifting my head to ensure eye contact.

"Okay Vic, calm down. I am not going to tell you with everyone else, because you deserve the right to know this information first." "Know what information Pierre? We don't keep secrets! What the hell is going on?" My questions spewed like daggers destined for penetration through the heart.

Pierre's voice deepened. "My love let me finish. I knew that Joshua had some less than stellar business dealings, but I never suspected anything of this magnitude." "Magnitude? What magnitude Pierre get to it already."

"I am trying Vic. Listen." "Okay." "I am a trader, there are business dealings that I have that you should not be privy too, and that is why I didn't think too deeply into what Joshua was doing. He is a real estate guru, Vic, and therefore he intermingles with billionaires and many types around the world. Arms dealing is extremely lucrative and doubly dangerous. If he was mixed up in anything like this, which evidence is pointing towards, there is a whole other person in Joshua, we've yet to meet."

"There's more Pierre, I know it. I feel you holding back, there are miles between us, yet our hands embrace. Please, the one thing that has never wavered between us is loyalty and trust. Whatever it is, we are in this together, we vowed forever. Talk to me Pierre."

"Vic, I put on a front for the others because I don't know how we can break this information to Sade. Joshua may very well be involved in illegal and dangerous activities, but even worse, I've discovered that he has another life, and before you ask, no I haven't seen him or talked to him." "What do you mean another life! He has a life here with my sister. Am I in the twilight zone or something? You can't be serious Pierre!"

Nodding his head assuredly, Pierre continued. "Oh my love, I am heart-wrenchingly serious. Javier and I are the only two people who are aware. He only knows because he helped me uncover mountains of secrets and lies that Joshua or whomever he is has kept hidden. After further investigation Javier was able to prove without a doubt, that Joshua has another woman and a son, that looked to be around five years old."

My mouth dropped open and my eyes felt like they bugged out of the socket. Did he just say another life, woman and a son?

"What?" "Yes, Vic, Joshua has been lying since the beginning. His business dealings afford him the opportunity of continuous travel. It is quite easy for him to have a family in another country and the two never cross paths. However, his business dealings have now exposed far more than he bargained for. Joshua has laid down with the wrong devil and now his sins are a rising inferno."

"Who is this other woman Pierre? And a son? Really?" "This woman, Victoria, is the daughter of the Sicilian arms dealer Javier told us about." "Does she have a name Pierre?"

"Her name is Annastasia Lea. Angelo's wife, Annastasia's mother, was killed five years ago. The case was never solved, at least not legally. There is no record of anyone being charged with her murder. I don't have all the answers, but looking at the timeline of Joshua entering our lives, and comparing that with when his time seems to end in their lives is fishy. My first wonder is if he had anything to do with the murder of his son's grandmother. There has to be a deep seeded reason for someone to completely try to reinvent themselves."

I was still, frozen. How the hell am I supposed to explain this to Sade? Who have we let into our world? How did we not see this coming? I loved him like a brother. His tenure in our lives has been a masquerade. Letting out a sigh, tears began to well in my eyes as Javier came aboard.

"Javier, I'm glad you made it safely." "Everyone's inside Vic, wondering if you two are okay and what's going on. I assume Pierre has filled you in. I know it's a lot to comprehend all at once, but we have to be strong for Sade."

I knew Javier had my sister's best interest at heart. His words were laced with sincerity and genuine concern. I listened. "I have more news and this will shatter her world. Joshua's real name is Antonio Ricci. And according to Sicilian documents I've been able to get my hands on, they were married. I have yet to find a record of divorce, further making his life with Sade a temporary lie of sorts. He can add polygamy to what lies beneath. Just know that when we approach this with Sade there are so many holes and variables we must be clear that we don't have all the answers. Our number one priority is Sade and the twins' safety, as well as the safety of the entire family."

You could feel the love in Javier's tone as he spoke of protecting my sister. "Thank you Javier for all that you've done to help us with this case. I know you were going to involve the police or FBI further once you had more solid information. Are we there yet? Do you have enough to call in the favor you mentioned? I know you're no longer with the Bureau but if it weren't for your knowledge we would still be waiting with zero leads or answers." "Yes Vic, I contacted my former partner and set everything in motion. They are aware that I am working with the family privately and are willing to work with me pooling our efforts to find Joshua, I mean Antonio."

Now for the hardest conversation I know I have ever had, I pray for strength. I must be strong enough for the both of us. I have to tell my sister that the last years of her life have been a lie, and the only real part of her life with the man she thought was her husband is that she actually gave birth to twins. The nerve of him to name one of his children after his first and from what it seems, only wife.

My heart is breaking into a trillion pieces just thinking about Sade's feelings and reaction. She deserves to know now. As I headed towards the house, Pierre and Javier followed close behind.

# Chapter Nine - Betrayal

My girls were sitting seemingly waiting for me to come into the house. As I walked in Sade looked up at me and immediately read the terror on my face. "What is it?" Sade spoke barely catching her breath, asking again. "What is it Vic?" All I could do was hold her. And I did.

Rae broke the silence. "Vic, we have to hear what happened so we know what we are dealing with here. I know this is difficult, but" - I interrupted. "But Sade deserves to know the truth. You've never been more right in your life Rae."

With no easy way to rip the bandage off my sister's heart, I blurted out, "Joshua's real name is Antonio Ricci. He is the son-in-law of Angelo Lea."

Sade pushed away from me with a vengeance and began spewing questions a mile a minute. "What do you mean? Son-in-law? Who is he married to?" I continued. "Yes, and he has a five year old son named Antonio Lea Ricci."

My sweet Sade was devastated. "A son. When? How? Why? I don't understand any of this. How could I have not known about his other life?

Where do they live? Oh HELL NO! Is that who had the audacity to call me about the ransom?"

By now Sade was wound up beyond recognition. She was ready to obliterate anything in her way.

Javier interrupted, careful to gauge Sade's demeanor. "Did you ever suspect anything dear?" Sade looked him in his eyes and said, "I'll kill him."

Her tone was hushed, calmed and instantly subdued. Her anger sheathed only to those that do not know the Sade that I know. Not a good sign. I am not the only one holding a secret from past blackouts, Sade too shares space in pandora's box that together we love to hate.

I can't understand why he chose my sister to start a new life with. Joshua was the love of Sade's life, after the death of her high school sweetheart, she never really opened up to another man before Joshua, or Antonio that is. The red in her eyes says it all.

Cher stood up, took Sade by the hand and motioned for us to follow her outside. The men stayed behind to give us some girl time. Sade immediately let go. Sade's only communication for twenty-two minutes was crying and nodding her head as we each tried to say whatever we could to ease the pain that we know would never leave. She is tied to this imposter for the rest of her life.

Sade cleared her throat and Rae asked Sade if she had ever suspected Joshua of cheating. Sade held her head low and yelled. "NO! I trustingly thought I was the love of his life. It never dawned on me that he was with another woman let alone married with a child. Shit I'm the other woman it seems. After losing my high school sweetheart many years ago and dealing with the demons that have plagued me due to the brutal rape I endured, I just knew the worst that could happen to me in my life, had already occurred. And now this!"

Rae moved closer up behind Sade just to further remind her that she has her back. Sade was in her head and while she knew we were there, I could tell she felt like she was on an island alone seeking a lifeline. I've been there several times. *I am my sister's keeper.*

Sade let it all out. "And no I don't want to talk about the fucking rape! Don't ask! Now I got this bitch, Annastasia stalking and blackmailing me. She knew how to find me. I feel it in my bones, it was her on the other end of that ransom call. Does she think I know where he is? Are they both trying to swindle me out of money?"

I am in a state of shock right now. Rae and Cher are sending me looks that could slice me in half with one too many blinks. For the first time since the day it happened, Sade has told someone, shit six people now know about her darkest hours. Conveniently, she closed her outburst demanding no follow-up questions, so everyone's mind is running a mile a minute. As the memories boil in my gut, I try to focus on Javier.

Javier explained that Angelo's mother was killed five years ago, and her murder has yet to be solved. Hindsight is twenty-twenty, I know that's around the time that Joshua came into our lives. "He didn't just get over on you sis, he pulled the wool over all of our eyes for quite some time. We don't know if he's disappeared because he fears for his life, or if he's fine and in cahoots with the Lea family." My blood was boiling over, churning at the thought of his existence.

Sade's eyes narrowed and her voice fell two octaves lower than normal. "That son of a bastard! Vic, he had the audacity to name my daughter after those people. After his first, I mean his only wife. Joshua, Antonio, what the fuck ever, he is going to wish we never met when I get through with his ass." "I am my sister's keeper, and you're damn right sis, he is going to wish he never met either of us!" And like clockwork, Cher came through with a verse from Queen Bey. *"Hot sauce in my bag, swag."*

Right now Sade is furious and that's the only emotion functioning. Cher led the way as we went back inside to see what the game plan was. Pierre, Matthew, Javier and Stephen were sitting in the cigar den drinking whiskey when we walked in to join them. Sade doesn't smoke, but Pierre already had one cut for me, Rae and Cher. We really hadn't taken a full tour of the estate, but we all know anywhere Cher goes, an in home cigar lounge must follow.

Matthew pulled Cher close and took the lead. "Okay ladies, it's time to get real. We have to put the emotions on the shelf and remain focused. An agent will be coming to the house to speak with us. Javier felt it best we speak in person. Face-to-face leaves less room for miscommunication of any kind. Stephen is taking me to meet with his contact in a few minutes. I am purchasing some weapons. I didn't have a chance to bring any from my arsenal and I will not be here unprotected depending on anyone else. No offense Javier." Nodding, Javier understood exactly what Matthew meant.

None of us objected, we'd never put more trust in law enforcement than we would in ourselves. With the training and years of experience in battle and enduring in situations most can only imagine, the men we love are who we trust first.

Matthew was a sniper, retired from the United States Army and he doesn't speak on it often. I think we are about to see him in action. Before leaving with Javier, he spoke with Pierre, leaving him the code for the safe and letting him know there's a gun inside fully loaded.

Matthew joined the service at a young age, and served twenty-five years before retiring. He is currently contracted by the government to perform special operations. It's the one part of his and Cher's relationship that is not transparent. Most of his operations are confidential. We all know it's for Cher's best interest.

Our strong intelligent men are truly a force to reckon with, especially when they are working together. Matthew would rather people not know of his innate skill set. The only reason we know is because of Cher. Out of respect for his privacy, it's discussed if he initiates the conversation. Otherwise there's no mention of his work.

Matthew kissed Cher, placed his hand on Rae's arm and spoke to his number one pupil with sheer confidence. "You've got the best aim of the group, here's my rifle. Become one with it just like during our lessons. Breathe, block out everything and feel the target. I need your help sis. You can handle it!" Rae took the rifle from Matthew's grip, and assured Matthew that she and Pierre could handle things while he was out.

Stephen kissed Rae with the most intense passion, looking into her eyes, he spoke with the deepest sincerity. "Follow your instincts my shield-maiden, I love you."

Stephen and Rae started taking shooting lessons with Matthew as a part of their exercise routine. They already box together and Rae always wanted to learn to shoot. She was overly excited when Stephen paid for them to take lessons from Matthew. Rae was a natural and has continued her lessons as a part of her regular weekly schedule.

Pierre locked the door behind Stephen. Cher got up and worked on what she could control, cooking.

Pierre and Rae took a detailed tour of the estate, careful to pay close attention to every door and window.

"We should be receiving another call. I don't know when, but the woman (*possibly Antonio's wife*) that called about the ransom said a call would come the next day with details. I wish I could slice Annastasia's jugular for putting my big sister through this bullshit. I wish Joshua would show his face and deal with us like a man."

"Nothing yet." Javier's voice jolted me out of my murder scene.

Javier said in his experience the call will come early afternoon. I didn't ask why, I was just grateful that it bought us a little time to prepare. After combing the inside of the home, Pierre asked Rae to stay inside with us, while he went to check the exterior of the property and remaining grounds. Pierre wanted to secure as much as possible and become familiar with his surroundings.

Javier and Matthew have been gone for about an hour, they should be returning soon. My nerves are better when we're all together.

Sade was entranced in thought, and I couldn't stop staring at her, wondering what must be going through her mind every second. Cher came into the living room and told us to all come into the kitchen to eat something.

Grilled grouper and blackened Mahi were our protein choices for this morning's brunch. We had buffalo cauliflower and zucchini which was absolutely delicious. Cher and Matthew caught a few fish on their last fishing trip and froze them when they came to the island to check on the property. Thank goodness, because we are all starving after the night we had and the ridiculousness we've had to mentally digest.

Just before sitting down to eat we heard what sounded like a motor. Rae immediately stood and followed Pierre to the door. As they approached, Javier flung it open, peeped in and asked Pierre to come help them bring everything inside.

After fifteen minutes of unloading, the guys took all the weapons into Matthew's artillery room. Returning to the kitchen, they sat down to eat. Matthew asked Pierre if he noticed any concerns as he swept the grounds. Pierre and Rae let him know that everything seemed normal from their perspective except the sliding glass door in the master sweet. That was the only entrance they noticed unlocked.

"Everything was phenomenal Cher, as always. Your cuisine is truly food for the soul. Now I wish it could grant me superpowers so I could cut straight to the core of all this bullshit my sister is enduring." Cher smiled. "I feel you Vic, you're welcome."

Javier patted me on the side of my left shoulder and began to explain what was going to happen next. "My contact will be here to meet us in fifteen minutes. I have him coming to the east guest house. It's the most secluded on the property. I want no one in this house besides us, and Matthew agrees. Although we are gaining inside intel, do not discuss what we have as protection in this home. We are dealing with an international arms dealer and we are not leaving our fate up to local law enforcement. While I respect their will to serve, it's not enough for what we could be up against." Javier was right, we truly could only trust ourselves at this point, so no need to elaborate with outsiders.

As Javier continued to explain, I could only think of the many ways I'd love to torture Annastasia for waging an attack on my sister. "Pierre and Matthew will come with me to meet with the FBI contact. Stephen is working on monitoring all traffic on and off of the island. Rae, keep the rifle and do sweeps of the rooms every thirty minutes while we are gone."

Javier leaned in closer, nodding his head ensuring the necessity of his requests. "Cher, Vic and Sade, we need you to comb through the files I have left on the desk in the cigar lounge. Look for anything that could lead us to the whereabouts of Annastasia Lea. After that, help Sade look into her assets and see if Joshua has accessed anything outside of the bank accounts, which he hasn't touched. I do know that Angelo has an estate off the coast in Trapani, Sicily, and it is possible that Annastasia has fled there with her son. All answers are up in the air."

I began to hear static in my head, feeling like Carol-Ann, stuck inside the television searching for the light in Poltergeist. I am trying my hardest to focus on what Javier is saying, fighting the blackout that is looming.

"Joshua could be there with her either willingly or by force. We honestly don't even know if he is alive. What we do know is that Joshua is associated with a very dangerous family, and in my years of training, preparedness trumps everything. Nonetheless, we must use our time wisely, and once all is complete we will reconvene. The calls to this estate are rerouted to my cell, so when the ransom call comes in, I won't miss it. I love you all."

The rest of us were trying so hard to focus on Javier's every word, we hadn't noticed Sade slip into the cigar lounge without us.

# Chapter Ten - Smoke & Mirrors

After two hours of searching and Rae keeping guard, Sade found something useful. An insurance policy was initiated on both my sister and the children for 2.5 million dollars each. Sade assured us she was not aware that Joshua had taken out an additional insurance policy. Next, Cher and I discovered there was a safety deposit box here on the island in his name, of which Sade also had zero knowledge of.

I sent Javier a text to tell him we found some information that could be useful. Javier responded letting us know they'd be returning to the main house soon. So we kept digging, and there in plain sight, I noticed it. As my sister's passport fell to the floor I leaned over picked it up and saw that Joshua's had flipped open. Letting out an excruciating gasp, I looked up at Sade in shock. The passport in my hand read Antonio Ricci, not Joshua Newman. As I stood to my feet I heard the door open, the men must have returned.

Storming out of the office, Sade throws the passport into Javier's chest. As if looking for instant answers. "What the hell is this shit Javier? We discovered a passport in Antonio Ricci's name, a safety deposit box in Joshua Newman's name and an insurance policy totaling 7.5 million dollars taken out on me and the children. Why would he do this? What did I do to deserve this besides love him? Was he planning to kill me and our children? I mean, how else could he cash in on the insurance policy? I don't understand. How did I not see this coming? I have been sleeping with the enemy for years without a clue." Javier grabbed Sade by the arms and pulled her in close. As the sobs grew louder the echo of why resounded.

We all gathered around Sade and Javier began to step back. Javier explained, "I need to go look at the safety deposit box information, there is still enough time to make it to the bank before it closes. Sade, I am here for you, but I have to keep working. I can't stop now." Looking at Cher, we both turned to him mouthing, "We got her." He nodded and stepped back into the cigar lounge.

Matthew motioned for Rae to walk the grounds with him and do another sweep of the property. I could tell by the look in his eyes there was something more brewing in his mind. Pierre and Javier went through all the information and took what they had and went to the bank to attempt opening the safety deposit box. Stephen's contact on the island happens to be on the board of trustees for the bank and has called in a favor. Javier and Pierre should be able to get in with no problem.

Sade's sobs began to soften eventually and just like that, her mood shifted from black to red. Walking to the kitchen she looked back, motioning for us to join her. Three shot glasses and one liter of whiskey. Sade poured, and we drank.

Five shots in, locked and loaded. "Alright Motherfucker I'm done crying and I am threw playing the victim. It is no accident that you were married and forgot to mention it. So yes, I'm infuriated at the thought of your continued existence." For a minute, Sade was speaking to the sky as if Joshua could hear her loud and clear.

Now looking at the rest of us with pain in her eyes she continued. "I was never more than an escape from hell's gate, but I refuse to let him skate his fate." Her eyes back on high, I looked at my sister and I knew her, no one else did in that moment but me. Pandora's box was prying open and will be stopped by nothing or no one. Winking towards the ceiling as if Joshua was listening, she walked off chanting. "He will wish he never knew me!"

Matthew and Rae had been gone for a while before we were rattled from the depths of our thoughts. We heard a shot. Startled, Cher ran to the window to see what was happening. Rae motioned for us to stay inside and to lock the doors. Rae and Matthew then disappeared out of view. The next ten minutes felt like an eternity, sitting, waiting in silence, and then the door flung open. It was Javier and Pierre. In unison we both let them know that we heard a shot fired.

Javier and Pierre split up, each taking a wing of the estate inside making sure there were no breeches. I grabbed Cher and Sade's hands and took them to the arsenal. We each got a piece and waited, ready and able. Pierre and Javier came back, nothing seemed out of place, but Matthew sent a text to Pierre and Javier telling them to come to the guest house.

As they were leaving Rae walked back in. "What was that?" Cher screamed. Sade looked into Rae's eyes, and before Rae could say a word, Sade shouted, "She's here, isn't she Rae? She's here! Right? Tell me please. You saw her. I feel it. That bitch is here Rae!"

Taking a deep breath, Rae hugged the rifle and screamed, "I shot someone! I don't know who he was. I caught him peering into the guest house window where Javier met the agent earlier. He didn't lower his weapon or back off when I approached so I shot that Motherfucker."

"Is he dead? I interrupted. "I don't know Vic!" Rae blurted out her words fiercely as she cocked the rifle again and continued. "I barely got a good look at his face. Matthew dragged him into the guest house." "Okay so if you didn't recognize him then it couldn't have been Joshua." "I don't know Vic, when he seemed as if he was raising instead of lowering his pistol, and refused to respond, I went red."

"Where's Sade?" Cher looked puzzled walking back towards the front of the house. "She was just here a minute ago, we were so busy staring at Rae we missed her slipping out again." Sade nowhere to be found is not good for anyone right now. I know my sister.

"Shit! I can't have my big sister roaming around here alone. I need her in my sights. You all have no idea what she's capable of at this point. I think she's let go of any ounce of reasoning. This is so much to process with basically no concrete information. I need to know what was found in the safety deposit box. The suspense is killing me. Now, we may have a dead body on our hands and no one knows who he is." I downed two more shots of liquid courage letting the charcoaled mellowed flavor linger on my palate appreciating the vanilla notes. I remind myself to breathe.

I text Pierre for answers fifteen minutes ago and he's just sending a response back.

> *Sade is here with us. I'm guessing no one saw her slip out. She saw the body, It is not Joshua, but looks shockingly just like him. He is not dead, barely speaking or moving, but still breathing. I can't make Sade leave at this point, but I need the rest of you to hang tight. I don't want you to witness Matthew, Javier or me doing what is necessary to get the information we need out of this son of a bastard. I love you and I need you all to stay put. Don't answer any calls and don't open the doors.*

Just as I was about to put my phone down, the landline rang. I thought Javier rerouted the calls to his cell. And Pierre just asked us not to answer the phone. What if it's the ransom caller?

I text Pierre back to tell him the phone was ringing. Javier came rushing into the house as I was pressing send. He said his phone was jammed for some reason he wasn't receiving a signal. By the time Javier got there the ringing had ceased.

I have to know, what was in the safety deposit box and who the hell is that man in the east guest house? My racing thoughts were halted by the phone ringing again.

Cher grabbed my hand and Javier picked up the receiver placing the call on speaker. "Hello his voice echoed. A woman was on the other end. "Your time is up, we are ready to set up a meet for the ransom. We know you're on the island and we know you've captured one of our men. Bring him unharmed to the meet with the money and no one has to get hurt. The location will be forwarded to Sade via text tonight and you will have thirty minutes from the time of the message to arrive at the location." Before any of us could get a word in edgewise, the call ended.

At a loss, Rae questioned the callers demands. "Why would we return the bastard to his people after he tried to harm us? Hell no, who does that? Fuck them and their rules! Why are they in control? Are we fighting for Joshua, I mean Antonio? Why? He's obviously a lying, cheating narcissist."

"This entire ordeal is crazy Rae, I know, but I have to try to keep a level head for my sister. What if they really are holding Joshua?"

Cher gave me the side eye and cut me off demanding our attention. "What if Joshua is actually the main character and culprit behind all of this bullshit Vic?"

God Rae is right, what if he is a lying, cheating narcissist like she suggested? I love Cher and Rae for always having my back.

Javier brought a box over to the table and sat it before us. "What is this?" The room fell silent as everyone awaited the answer to my question.

"This came from the safety deposit box. I have already shown Sade the contents. Just more doubt and confusion compounded by unending deceit have arisen. Right now she sees the man in the guest house as her only tangible asset to receive answers."

Javier's eyes dropped low for a moment before continuing. "Your sister is hurting on so many levels right now, we just have to be a little patient with her. I think that we are going to discover the truth soon. The walls are closing in on the Leo family and one of Stephen's contacts saw a woman fitting Annastasia's description coming off of a yacht near the Leo estate. I have a feeling this man's appearance on Cher's property and Annastasia's return to the island are no coincidence."

One day we are all living our lives without a care and the next we have no clue which way is up. My psyche is exhausted and my heart hurts an indescribable pain. Numbness is setting in and in this moment all I can do is open the box, hoping for answers.

Rae sat next to me. We opened the box together, and my phone rang. It's Pierre. Before I could say hello, he asked, "Is your sister there?"    I immediately responded. "No, I thought she was with you. What do you mean is she here Pierre?"

"She said Cher text her to come back to the house and she was headed there. I told her to send me a message when she got there because Matthew and I don't want to leave this asshole in here unattended.   Besides, I'm far from through with his ass.   He's going to wish Rae killed him." "Okay well, my sister isn't here Pierre! My scream echoed sending a chill through the air."

Javier took the phone from me and put it on speaker.  "Hey man its Javier, I will go out and check the property."

"I can't believe this. Where is my sister? What is she thinking?  Who could have called that would make her leave the guest house and lie to us? What if it was Joshua or Annastasia?"   Rae placed my hand in hers and began to squeeze, trying to calm my nerves. My head is in turmoil from overthinking and seeking answers when I have so little to go on. These last couple of days have been like a nightmare that won't end. I keep trying to wake up but I can't.

Javier closed the box and we all stood up. He went outside to look around the property, while Cher, Rae and I combed every inch of the house again. We found no sign of Sade. Now I'm scared. What if they kidnapped her or killed her and already dumped her in the Atlantic? Rae grabbed my chin and dared me to snap out of it. She knew my thoughts were diving into the darkness. Rae was in big sister mode now, her voice commanding. "Do as I say, boss up and put on the gloves."

## Sade

*I know I shouldn't but my heart can't help it. His voice commanded to see me. Hearing Sade roll off the tip of his tongue in his familiar endearing tone gave me chills. I know everyone is going to be angry and concerned about me sneaking away, but I have to go. Joshua or Antonio or whomever, called. I know his voice, he was the love of my life for years. He asked me to meet him at Cher's restaurant. He told me to come alone and all I can think about is getting answers. My babies and our future flashing before my eyes.*

Javier came running back into the house. "I didn't see her anywhere, and one of Cher's cars are gone." Completely forgetting about going through the safety deposit box, I darted out of the house and let out a scream that should have raised the dead around the universe. Over and over and over and over, I whaled until Cher came and wrapped her arms around my body holding me tight. Swaying from side to side. All I could do was cry.

Stephen walked up with dinner and drinks for everyone as Rae was coming to help Cher with me. He put the food down and came back to the front, nodded for Rae and Cher to back away and he picked me up, my body almost completely limp.

He laid me on the chaise and knelt before me. "Vic you have to breathe. This is bigger than all of us. I have been doing a lot of digging and calling in a host of favors. Joshua was never who he said he was. I believe he murdered Angelo Leo's wife, his real wife's mother." "He's a murderer? Stephen we've allowed a monster to come into our lives and not one of us saw through his loving façade."

We are living in a nightmare and I don't know how to save my sister from her heartbreaking reality. Stephen softened his stare knowing my thoughts were running into a brick wall, fear.

"Vic, Evidence is leading me to think that once he killed her he faked his death and assumed another identity. He somehow thought he could start over and no one would ever recognize him or connect him to his past. Relocating from Trapani, Sicily, to south Florida may have worked if the Leo family didn't have property in Miami. Perhaps Joshua never considered that in his haste to transition. Between his business dealings and our current social media age, he should have known he couldn't remain a ghost forever."

With a baffled look on his face, Stephen continued. "Perhaps he really fell in love with your sister, wanted to start over and attempt to live happily ever after, but all that has backfired. Whatever he was thinking was never actually going to work. He's a murderer, or at least the Leo family believes he is and now they obviously know he is still alive. They are coming after all that he has, and that includes Sade and her family."

Javier returned shortly after. Matthew and Pierre came back into the house. Their pale faces held a story I was afraid to hear. Picking up my husband's hands, I squeezed, and I knew. The mystery man was dead. Matthew's hands were worse than Pierre's, bruised and battered. I had no desire to see what the inside of the east guest house looked like. I could only imagine.

Cher locked eyes with Matthew and him the spare set of keys to the car that Sade took. She also gave him access to the GPS tracking on the car. Javier messaged his FBI contact and had them on standby to meet us when necessary. They were already closing in on a case regarding the Leo family so this is just adding more fuel to the fire.

Rae stood up and disappeared into the cigar lounge. Cher followed to check on her while all I could do was hold Pierre's hands and lean into his chest. What started out as anniversary bliss has turned into lies, murder and deceit. And now my husband was running on sheer adrenaline.

# Chapter Eleven - Lone Rider

## Sade

*I remember my parents always telling me they named me after their favorite singer, Sade. The mellow vibes of her artistry are not taking over me at this moment. I feel I may end up doing their musical 'idol' a great injustice. Her flow is the epitome of grace and serenity. Her music makes your soul speak, and her energy is freeing. I was thirteen the first time our parents took us to her concert at Madison Square Garden. Reminiscing on happier days helps me breathe, because right now I feel as if someone has a chokehold on me while stabbing repeatedly, the hollow hole in my chest.*

Sade knows that I love her, yet she also knows that I know her deepest thoughts better than anyone. She is surrounded by loved ones, yet feeling isolated, violated and over exposed. Her heart is burning with pain and her thoughts are laced with unending questions.

With the GPS tracker on our side, Matthew and I have almost caught up to her. I pray we arrive soon, I know she is armed and I know her vision is clouded. I feel the turmoil of yesteryear's buried manipulation and rape creeping into the energies surrounding the halo we've graciously welcomed for years. Channeling all of our secrets and familial indiscretions hidden in the pastures of old times, we vowed to forgive ourselves for allowing vulnerability to lead us to prey. Yet now, here we are, out of the mouth of the whale and into the lion's lair.

Fearlessness has overwhelmed her soul and all she knows is survival. She is a warrior. A mother's love has taken over as we promised to each other. No one would ever violate our children the way she had been raped of innocence, and left to cover it up as if nothing ever happened.

### Sade

*I am his Sade, I am the love of his life, or so I thought. I gave him the precious gift of two beautiful children, and I have supported his entrepreneurial goals at every turn, emotionally and financially. How could I have been so naïve. I should have known, I don't know how, but I should have known.*

*I learned on the night of my rape that I was an insignificant tool to the male species. I should have never given in to love, or the excruciating pain that is served with it. Everyone will be furious with me. I have no idea if I am making the correct decision, but I must see Joshua's face. I have to see if he is okay, hurt or under duress. Thoughts racing and raging these last years all seem like a lie, and I have no understanding as to why. Why me? What will I do when I lay eyes on him finally? Since my first love passed, Joshua has been the only other soul I've let my guard down for. How could I not know who my own husband was? Was he even my husband? No!*

*My foot pressed against the pedal burning a hole in the floor. Before I noticed it, I was driving over one hundred miles an hour on Fisher Avenue. I could see the sign for the restaurant in the distance. Nervous anger now consumed me.*

Releasing my foot from the pedal, the car glided until the sign was in full view.

Turning in, I see the silhouette of a man's shadow coming from around the side of the building. Now in plain sight, he is alive. The tears welled in my eyes began to free fall uncontrollably. Shock settled in. Just then, another man identical to the one before me came from behind the building and stood next to Joshua. Were there three of them? The man from the guest house scarily resembled Joshua, and now these two. I shook my head, rubbed my eyes and blacked out.

When I came to, dark cinder walls surrounded me, and as my vision came into focus I saw Joshua sitting over me. Startled I jumped back only to find that my feet were literally chained to the wall. In an instant I began to scream so uncontrollably until I felt the tightening of hands shaking me free. My sister and Matthew screaming for me to awaken. In that moment I realized that the chains were a nightmare and Joshua or his clones were nowhere to be found.

*He must have noticed someone following me and ran once I passed out.*

"Sis, there were two of them. I mean the dead guy from the guest house and now the two men that approached me upon arrival. They all look undeniably like Joshua or Antonio's clone." As the words escaped Sade's lips her eyes grew more confused.

Matthew looked me in my eyes and asked me to let go. I stepped aside and let him take over. "Why would you come alone? Javier and the rest of us agreed we need to stay together and you definitely shouldn't be going anywhere alone. I hate what this is doing to you, but we have no idea how deep Joshua is in this. I am pleading with you to come back with us." Sade simply nodded and went limp into Matthew's arms.

Backing out of the driveway, I noticed a silhouette in my rearview. Slamming the breaks, I let out a fierce scream. Matthew's head flew forward then backward uncontrollably. Following my stare, he jumped out of the car. Sade then whispered in a hushed tone, "Joshua?" It was as if she was asking a question. Her eyes were filled with confusion. Immediately I sent Cher, Rae, Javier, Pierre and Stephen a group text letting them know Joshua was at the restaurant. With no time to type I just told them to get here now.

Unbeknownst to me, Javier had a tracker on the car Matthew and I were using so they pulled up behind us less than a second after I sent the message. Javier and Pierre flew out of the car before Rae put it in park. Rae leaned over grabbed the sawed off shotgun from beside her left foot and stood aiming straight for Joshua's head.

Joshua stood there now with his hands raised and began to plea. He dropped to his knees and begged Sade to speak with him alone. Cocked and loaded, Rae blurted out obscenities. "Hell no motherfucker! She goes nowhere with you!"

Javier and Pierre grabbed each side of Joshua and told him to walk. They disappeared inside the restaurant, leaving Rae zoned and Sade frozen within her thoughts. I loosened my grip slightly and, Sade took off into the restaurant. I started to follow until I heard the sounds of gunshots. I turned around and Rae was at my side in a flash. She threw a nine millimeter my way and we approached the door slowly. Hearing sirens in the near distance, I figured Javier must have alerted his FBI contact.

Rae and I walked slowly towards the door and were halted just as I put my hand on the knob by more shots fired. Rae placed her hand atop of mine and together we eased the door open. Creeping through the door it was pitch dark inside and smelled of fresh blood and stale cigars.

I could hear Pierre talking to Javier, but couldn't make out what was being said. Then I heard a strange voice chime in. Rae and I stopped in our tracks. Listening carefully, we could hear Sade weeping, asking why, repeatedly. The closer we got, the louder her sobs echoed. Seeing no one, I figured they must be in the kitchen. Just as I was about to push the kitchen door open, I heard Rae's wrist pop in the death of silence and boom, back to back, two shots were fired. Just over my shoulder, her aim was impeccable.

Who was this man? I could barely see, but he too looked just like Joshua. Another clone. This now makes two men killed that look like my sister's husband. Sade was not hallucinating. I may have passed out too when I pulled up for a secret meeting with my missing husband, and was confronted with a mangy look alike.

"He was aimed at my head, it was either kill or be killed. Matthew said if anyone pulls a gun, only assume that they intend to use it and use mine faster. So I did." Rae spoke in a matter-of-fact tone, making it clear she'd do it again. Rae grabbed my hand squeezing hoping to calm my nerves. Pierre and Javier flung through the kitchen door and when I didn't see Sade, my eyes fell low, my heart sank and then I heard my name. My sister was alive.

Matthew placed his hand on Rae's and slid the shot gun from her grip, pulled her in and said, "I am grateful for you." Letting out an abysmal sigh, Rae assured, "I got you."

Sade came slowly into view with hands outstretched, covered in blood and death's remnants smeared all over her shirt. Rae and I turned to her and she landed between the two of us and buried her head in the safety of our embrace.

Looking up with barely enough breath left, Sade's voice began cracking through the tears. "My children's father is dead. Joshua, Antonio, whoever he is, is gone. I gave up everything for him, and he had the nerve to threaten the safety of my children, my mother, my family and everyone I love, all to keep up his greedy whorish tendencies. He was a murderer and a snake."

My heart was pounding so hard it felt like it could be heard miles away. Without interruption, Sade continued. "Antonio is a triplet, and Annastasia was always the love of his life. He only left her, faked his own death and moved on because he needed to escape murder charges. She figured out somehow that he was alive and began pursuing his whereabouts until she found him. Annastasia had her father's goons kidnap him and the saga unfolds. She felt betrayed and abandoned. He killed her mother years ago. I don't know the details, or if I ever will. He did give me a key to a home here on the island. It is in our children's name. He told me there is where I will find the remaining answers governing his presence in my life. He then pulled his gun from under his shirt, apologized for never loving me enough, and shot himself in the heart first and then the head. Brain matter splattering everywhere, and my life flashed before my eyes."

We could hear the sirens outside as the door to the restaurant opened, we all turned around and held our hands high.

Rae's shots were solely in self-defense, and without her who knows if any of us would be alive in this moment. Rae turned to Javier and he placed his hand on her shoulder and told her not to worry. As her witness, her actions were justified and necessary considering their life threatening circumstances. Rae assured him that no matter what, there were no regrets. Rae said without hesitation, "I'd damn sure do it again! Thanks for having our backs Javier."

After speaking with the FBI for the next five hours, all of us were exhausted, and drained beyond comprehension.

Stephen and Cher stayed behind to keep an eye on the properties while we dealt with questioning. I called to fill them in as soon as we got on the road and they were impatiently awaiting our arrival. We were gone for hours, and I know the suspense was killing Cher. She made sure the Bourbon Princess was ready to go if and when needed, while Stephen had spent his time ensuring the property was secured.

Now the aftermath is before us.

# Chapter Twelve - The Lion's Den

Wound up so tightly, as exhausted as we were we couldn't sleep. I cuddled up next to Sade and held her tightly through the remaining of the night.

Pierre lay at the foot of the bed, fixated on us. Sade broke the silence and asked if the girls and I would go with her to the house. She needed to see what Joshua had left behind and more than half of her questions were still unanswered. Rae and Cher lifted their heads from the floor where they made themselves cozy. In unison, we all said, "Yes." Wanting to be near each other, there is no way Sade will be going to that house alone.

After months of longing for Joshua to return unharmed, Sade's life has been flipped upside down and inside out. Joshua's mask fell to the floor without warning and my sister's world will never be the same. I am not sure how she will ever trust another man again. After overcoming our childhood skeletons, and now this, I am not sure she will ever open up again. Another love taken from her, I can't expect her to allow that feeling to resurface. I wish her the strength to someday love once more, but I completely understand how this experience may have scarred her from letting love in.

I assume we all drifted off to sleep at some point, because when I woke to the aroma of fresh brewed coffee, I noticed I was in bed alone. The room was empty and immediately I called out for Sade.

Pierre opened the bathroom door and wished me a good morning. "Sade and the girls are downstairs in the kitchen having coffee and waiting for you to awaken, my love."

"Good morning Pierre. How does Rae seem today? We haven't even mentioned what she was forced to do last night. I don't want to think about what would have happened if her reflexes were not spectacular. I know her demons, and I don't want her to shy into her self-absorbed darkness after this." "I know babe, and we are all here for Rae and grateful for her quick draw. Matthew has obviously been an excellent teacher. I know Stephen is relieved that he agreed to take formal lessons as a couple with Matthew, never realizing how life enhancing those sessions would turn out to be."

Dressed and as ready as I'll ever be, I made my way downstairs to find everyone sitting around the table outside as if giving thanks for the air they still breathe.

When I opened the door, Sade stood and came to me. Nothing was said, we just hugged for minutes. I then pulled back slightly and asked her if she was ready to go to the house. She nodded yes and began to explain that we had to wait for Javier and Matthew to return from the property first. They refused to let us go without them, and they insisted on going there first to do a sweep of the property.

Matthew sent Cher  a text letting her know that they are headed back here now. Cher explained that the guys are going to follow us back to the house, and they will wait outside until we are ready to leave. I can't blame them for wanting to stay close to us.

Reading Sade's facial expressions and body language, I could visibly tell her spirit was numb.

Sade began speaking in a hushed tone and I just wanted to melt where I stood. "I am nervous. Not knowing what other lies are left unearthed is frightening and somewhat debilitating. I have literally lived a façade for the last five years and I hope you all will be here for me when I go home to explain to my children why their father will never return to them."

"My sweet Sade, it's Vic, you know I'm always here for you, we all are. My niece and nephew will want for nothing, and Pierre and I will do everything we can to support your needs. The children will have access to every resource they need without question or hesitation as long as they need it. Healing will be a process, not a sprint, and we are here for it!"

According to the directions, we should arrive at Joshua's within the next five minutes. Sweaty palms and dismantled thoughts lead the way as we approach the parking space. Rae suggested we wait. "I know the guys swept the place but something doesn't feel right to me. I am going in first. Vic, stay here with Sade and Cher. Keep your 'Betty' ready."

*Betty is the name we called guns because my father used to call his gun Betty.*

Stepping out of the car, Rae turned around and motioned for Matthew to let him know she was going in alone first. Rae was always the protector even when we are protecting her. It's just embedded in her soul. Watching Rae disappear around the side of the house sent chills down my spine.

Five minutes later Javier received a phone call. Startled, he pulled the phone from his ear to look at it strangely after hearing Angelo Lea's voice piercing through the other end.

Javier's face now a deepened red bursting with fury, as he promised, "I have involved the FBI and what you get away with now will haunt the hell out of you in the future. If anything happens to any of my people, I will hunt you down and gut you from your ass to your appetite! I will not be a pawn in your game of thrones. This is my family you have so eagerly fucked with!" Not moved in the least, Angelo hung up, but not before making it clear that his daughter had already received the ransom she requested and we could thank Antonio in his death for making sure it was paid.

In a daze, Sade said, "I think it's time! We need to go in behind Rae." The door was still ajar and it was quiet. Wondering why Rae didn't come back to let us know all was clear, I called out for her. Only silence answered. I motioned to the guys that Cher, Sade and I were going inside, they followed because Rae was unresponsive.

Vanilla and lavender scents filled my sinuses proving that this was definitely a place occupied by my ex brother-in-law. The lights were out so the place was pitch dark. Cher called out for Rae again and still no answer. My heart sank to the pit of my stomach and in the same breath I heard Sade gasp. Turning our heads in unison Cher and I both did the same. Feeling the warmth of Matthew, Pierre and Stephen walking up behind us, we were all shocked.

Sitting on the master bedroom bed was Annastasia Lea Ricci with a sawed off shotgun pointed at her right temple.

Point blank is the only range Rae cared about. Rae tilted her head to the side, looked at us, and sucked her teeth before making her demands. "Back the fuck up, all of you! This little Sicilian bitch thought she was going to catch up with my Sade alone. That's her piece over their on the floor. Goddamn dad's an arms dealer and this bitch is riding around with a 280! Really! I guess she thought Sade was going to stroll up in here naively without any support. Never on my watch!"

Stephen moved up a little closer and began to call Rae's name when I touched his hand and held it for a second. In this state Stephen has not seen Rae. She is completely gone at this point. Her senses and reactions are no longer her own. Her mind, body and soul are fueled solely by the will to survive, and for good reason! Many years ago she vowed never to let another attack her, or anyone she loves after once being breathless, and left for dead. Self-defense is her new sir name and she wears it confidently.

Nudging the rifle against Annastasia's temple, Rae demanded she start talking and leave nothing out. "You have a full audience and we have nowhere better to be. Start telling my Sade why you spent the last months harassing her instead of taking your issues up with your family! You felt the need to drag her through this nightmare. Why? Speak! You were full of demands on the phone and now, crickets! All bark and no bite, you trifling piece of shit!"

Sade began to take deep breaths that could be heard from miles beneath the earth. Sade was staring without void into the soul of the woman sitting before her as if willing Annastasia to speak. In a hushed and almost humbled tone, Annastasia began to talk.

"He was my husband." As the words spilled from Annastasia's lips, Rae pressed the rifle harder into her temple. Annastasia's voice began to crack in nervousness, yet she continued.

## Annastasia

Joshua's real name is Antonio, which I know you have already discovered. We were together longer than we were married. Never one to trust, having known Antonio and his brothers since childhood, we were friends, or so I thought.

Friends before lovers, I assumed made our relationship even more unstoppable. After Antonio left the Navy, we married, and moved to our new home gifted to us by my father in Trapani, Sicily. Both American born citizens, however we held an undying love for the Sicilian coast. For a while we were living in perfect bliss, or so I thought.

It's no secret what you think my father does for a living, but you have to understand, I will never say anything against him. Trying to make me would be futile. He was a provider, a father and a devoted husband until he discovered that my mother was having an affair with my husband. He's a fucking triplet looking identical to his brothers, my mother still chose him. Of all the sick and twisted things to do to another human, she did it without regret.

My mother was a gorgeous woman according to most. Tall and voluptuously proportionate, with thick brunette hair flowing past the small of her back. Naturally curly, she wore it straight. Her skin was a smooth olive and she looked best without makeup. A natural beauty with the confidence of a lion ready to feast. Her clothes draped with the flare of Jacqueline Kennedy Onassis. Most people assumed we were sisters.

Joshua and his brothers were not close, therefore when my father discovered the affair, he went to them first. He needed to gauge their loyalty, understanding that family comes first. Although the brothers don't get along personally, they have worked cohesively under my father for years. Professionally, Antonio, Dominick, and Demetri are excellent employees with a proven record of pleasing my father.

My father received a recording of my mother and Joshua having sex in every position one can think of for hours uninterrupted. Watching it repeatedly, my father had the image of my mother looking into the camera directly at the end of the porno and winking sheepishly, engrained in his memory.

Of course when I was told, I demanded to see the video myself. I couldn't believe it otherwise. I never trusted my mother, and our relationship has always been forced. However, this, I could have never imagined. When I reached the end of the video and saw the eye wink, I knew she was the woman behind the video delivery. It was my mother. She wanted to hurt my father in the worst way possible. It would have been so much easier to believe that this disgusting video was recorded by anyone else rather than his own wife. I knew deep down inside she hated me, but to have an ongoing affair with your daughter's husband is despicable.

Veronica was my stepmother since the age of eight. I was forced to call her mother. Coming into our lives less than two months after the questionable suicide of my biological mother, I was not permitted to speak of my biological mother around my father's new wife. Every memory of my birth mother was erased, and I was to move on with life without expressing feelings about her openly. This hardened my heart to his wife, but I acted respectfully because I refused to lose two parents. If putting up with her was necessary to remain at my father's side, then so be it. I did it.

Antonio came out of the womb a con artist, but I assumed because we knew each other on other levels, he wouldn't do me wrong. I let my guard down and fell into the deepest love of my life. When our son was born I thought we were destined to be together forever. Unbeknownst to me, I was just the cover for the true love of his heart. Veronica! That's why I took pleasure in telling that narcissist that I knew about his affair. I relished the look on his face, finding out that his beloved sent the video proof to my father to belittle my father's pride and shred his heart.

Of course Joshua did not find humiliating Angelo Lea a necessary action. He was furious. Miss Veronica did not have his permission to share the video with anyone. He was a babe in understanding the ways of the wicked stepmother of the south.  A selfish soul now with a husband and a lover feeling scorned.

In that moment Antonio realized he was only ever a pawn in her game to make my father lose control. Veronica sought attention, and attention she received. She never forgave my father for not wanting more children after they were married. He said I was enough and with the loss of my mother, he never wanted me to question his loyalty and love for me. More children would not make him any more whole he used to say, and Veronica cringed every time.

Hearing every word I was spewing his way, Antonio turned, mumbling obscenities completely zoned in a fury. Feeling validation rise, I let him go mourn the news that his lover was a trifling whore. Dealing with a kaleidoscope of emotions, it took me a minute to rev up and go after him.  Of course, by then he was gone without a trace.

No one heard from him for a couple of days, until detectives walked in while I was having dinner in one of my father's restaurants. Yes, he too owns Italian restaurants.

The detectives told my father that Veronica had been murdered, and without a chance to process the information, asked if we knew where Antonio was. Apparently detectives had him under surveillance for a while and knew about the affair long before we did. They have been following my father and his top men for months if not years. The detectives explained that witnesses confirmed hearing Antonio and Veronica arguing, and then the next morning, Veronica was found dead on the floor in the bathroom.

A month of searching for Antonio proved to unearth nothing. Everyone that was available to be questioned had alibis that checked out. Demetri and Dominick were prepared to stop their brother to prove their loyalty to my father. As their sole provider and male role-model since the age of thirteen, he was like their father too. Ultimately, they'd die to protect my father.

Receiving a tip that Antonio had been spotted at the airport, about to board a flight to Puerto Rico, with a five hour layover in Las Vegas, Nevada, the two brothers remained determined. With no clue if either place was Antonio's expected destination, Demetri and Dominick made it to the airport just in time to miss boarding. The flight had already pulled away from the hanger and was next in line on the runway for take-off. Prepared to follow on the next flight out, they waited impatiently, because one wasn't available until the next morning.

Later that evening the world watched in shock as the plane Antonio was supposedly on spiraled into the Mediterranean. We never heard from Antonio again. Reportedly there were no survivors, one hundred fifty-nine deaths.

Antonio was a ghost, until he became incomprehensibly cocky. I own a second home, small quaint place in Trapani overlooking the Mediterranean Sea. This space was a haven from our castle style home a little further inland. We used to spend weekends at our place on the coast and shut out the world for hours.

I only discovered he was alive because he made a drastic mistake. If you remember last year, Sade, Antonio brought you to the place in Trapani. I am sure he claimed to be treating you to a luxurious vacation. Filling the mold he engineered for himself as a so-called successful real estate guru. What he was unaware of is that I had the place completely wired with state-of-the-art security, equipped with one hundred percent video coverage. I left no space unmonitored.

Seeing you there with Joshua infuriated me. He robbed my son of a father in his cowardly escape from his former life. I don't know how he survived or if he was ever really on that particular flight to begin with, but I know it was him on that video waltzing around my place with you. I watched in hatred and disgust, the two of you seemed unmistakably happy.

This is where my desire for revenge was fueled and the rest is history. Antonio thought he could leave me here to pick up all the pieces without having to be held accountable for destroying my life in so many aspects. I never cared that he killed Veronica. Honestly, I was relieved she was gone from my father's life. I just wished my father never had to be plagued with such pain and humiliation.

You, Sade, became a casualty of war in my eyes. With no commitment to me I knew I shouldn't have misguided animosity towards you, yet I did. I studied you like a genius, and it was obvious you thought Antonio was truly who he remade himself to be. Only a small part of me cared that this wasn't your fault. Everyone in my path deserved to feel the excruciating pain boiling in my veins.

The ransom was because he took from me financially and emotionally. Antonio used the resources my family provided him in his former life to start anew, as if our son and I never existed.

He committed family treason. We gave him everything and treated him with love and respect from day one. This type of betrayal was death-worthy in our world, and I know that's exactly why he faked his death. He had no faith that I would plead on his behalf, and I honestly do not know if I would have.

Cher is a true sister to you Sade. She paid double the ransom amount, wiring ten million dollars to me, and swore herself to secrecy. I only had to agree to never contact you again. I agreed and put the money in a trust to add to my son's future inheritance. I should have stayed away, but I just had to see you and share all of this face to face.

Sighing in relief as if unburdening her soul, Annastasia lowered her eyes slightly and asked Rae if she could use the restroom. With the rifle sturdy against her temple, Rae looked over at Sade. Sade nodded in approval, and Rae jerked Annastasia from sitting.

Following her to the bathroom, Rae kept the rifle nestled in her slithering spine, yet Annastasia managed to find a window of opportunity to catch Rae off guard when reaching forward to open the bathroom door. Elbowing Rae in the eye, and kicking her in the throat in one swift kick, Annastasia tried to gain control of the situation.

A futile thought on her part, because before Annastasia's leg landed back in its proper position, we heard an explosion that haulted our movements. In shock we watched Annastasia fall to the floor. Pierre and Stephen opened fire simultaneously seeing only Rae's safety as the number one priority. Barely balancing herself, Sade picked up Annastasia's 280 and shot her again, with her own gun, piercing her heart at point-blank-range.

Breaths shallow and weak, Annastasia whispered, "Thank you for freeing me from this life of misery. You took everything from me and now I have destroyed your family. Antonio is dead and there is nothing left for me here. My father may never prove that Antonio killed my stepmother, but I know he did. She showed sheer disrespect and humiliated him on so many levels with the way the affair was exposed. My son deserves better than to have his parents mar the rest of his life. Thank you."

She wanted us to kill her after she freed her conscious. Wish granted.

There was never a letter or explanation as Antonio had expressed before he died. If there was, Annastasia must have removed it before we arrived. I'm not sure what closure if any a letter or more information from Antonio would bring. The man my sister met and married was Joshua. Joshua is dead. Annastasia and Sade are mourning two different men occupying the same body.

# Chapter Thirteen - After The Storm

Speaking to Cher and Rae, I felt a little disoriented. "Did all this really happen?" I heard the words seep from my mouth as if I were waiting for a response different from our reality. Annastasia and Antonio are both dead and now it's time to pick up the pieces. Maybe it's a blessing my niece and nephew are infants and oblivious to their father's antics.

Pierre drove our car back to Cher's and Javier drove the other car following us closely. Pierre touched my thigh gently and reminded me that he will always be here to protect me, Sade, the twins and my mother. He and Matthew both spoke out, reminding Sade that she will never be alone.

As soon as we got back to the house Cher exerted all of her anxious energy in the kitchen. Sade and Rae headed for the Whiskey and walked outside to sip and take in the night sky. I asked Rae if she was going to be okay. She nodded her head in assurance and said nothing.

From arms dealing to kidnapping and then murder. This is an unforgettable anniversary year for us.

Drifting in thought for a moment to the beautiful gesture of Pierre having my very own design brought to life and gifting it to me as an anniversary present made me smile inside. There was still some good that could be remembered from this anniversary. Rae and Cher stepping in and making the day even more special between catering, the yacht and a makeover from the miracle worker, left me with a few good memories to cherish from this year's anniversary.

Pierre and Stephen walked outside and turned on the music. I don't blame them for wanting to drown the conversations in their heads. There will surely be follow-up questions we may need to answer further with law enforcement. Javier took care of most of the statement information required. Everything done on our end was solely in self-defense.

Stephen sat down with a glass of Gentlemen Jack and shouted to the sky, "Fuck the world!" Sade had already downed two shots. I can't imagine what she is thinking. Her children and their entire life is starting over now, without a father.

Cher peeped her head out of the kitchen window to ask if we wanted to eat outside on the patio. In unison we responded, "Yes." Pierre went back inside to help Javier and Matthew bring the food outside. I helped Cher set the table, and we all sat together.

Before the questions turned into a deposition, Cher asked for everyone's attention.

### Cher

I know you're in shock after the ordeals we've risen through. I didn't expect you to discover that I paid the ransom. I humbly had no intention of telling you that I wired the money to Annastasia. She finally reached out again and while no one was paying attention I offered her a deal I thought she could not refuse. I would have given more if necessary. All I cared about was doing what was in my power to keep Leo and Lea safe first.

I offered the additional five million to the ransom trying to ensure that Annastasia would leave Sade alone, and allow her to move on with her life. I would give all I have for any one here right now. You all are my family and I pray you will always know that I too, am my sister's keeper. I don't want to speak about the money again, I don't want to hear how dangerous my decision was. I just want you to understand that I love you and there is absolutely nothing that will ever change that.

Tears welling in most of our eyes, we just sat there silently appreciating each other's presence. I looked at Sade and we both turned to Cher and said, "Thank you, sis." Sade then asked that we hold hands as she led us in prayer. Her words were many and her heart was open.

### Sade

Dearest Father, thank you for the blessings you have given to us. Thank you for bringing these souls into my life. Thank you for protecting my children and our lives through this ordeal. Please help me and all of us to understand the lessons and purpose for us having gone through these recent experiences. Thank you for allowing Pierre, Javier, Matthew and Stephen to prove to me despite my circumstances that good men still exist. Thank you for watching over my mother in my absence. Please give us the strength to continue carrying on in this life with forgiveness in our hearts. I pray for freedom from past and current pain. Thank you for Victoria. Thank you for giving me my precious little sister, my mini-me, my ride or die. This road ahead will be scary, but I will walk it with eyes wide open, in faith. I pray for everyone to have the perseverance to get beyond what has happened. Cher has opened her home and so much more to us. A true sister/friend, words can never express how grateful I am for you and Rae stepping in without hesitation to support us. I never could have imagined that this is how my marriage would turn out. No one could predict such circumstances. Through it all, I appreciate everyone at this table for putting your own lives on hold and being here for me. It may be a while before I feel any semblance of normalcy, but still I am grateful to you Father, for everyone's unwavering support. Okay, okay no more tears tonight, let's eat family.

After dinner, I called mom to see how things were at home. I didn't fill her in on the details, however I made sure she knew we were okay. I let her know we would all be returning within the next day or two. Eager to hug our necks, I could hear the relief in her voice. "We love and miss you mom, see you soon. Kiss the babies for us." I passed Sade the phone so she could speak with mom for a minute. When she was finished we went back outside with the others.

In need of easing the tension in my muscles, I turned on the hot tub and soaked my body. Sade, Cher and Rae joined me while the guys sat by the fire pit enjoying their cigars and whiskey, trying to clear their minds of the horror film our lives recently turned into.

"I've decided to return to work earlier than expected. I will be contacting the school when I get back to Miami to update my leave status. With the children's father gone, I don't have time to mope. I want to dive back into work and start to build a financial future for us. Sitting around the house will only keep me stagnant and constantly thinking about my loss. I don't want to make that my story, and I don't need to digress. Victoria, you know first-hand how dark my world can get, and I must control my emotions. The only way for me to do that effectively is to throw myself back into my work, my gardening and focusing on raising Leo and Lea."

I expect nothing less from my big sister. Sade is one of the strongest souls I know. "My warrior sister, yes, I completely understand and I support your decisions."

Sade explained that she would be hiring a nanny that we all interview and trust to ensure the perfect fit and choice for our family. "I will need everyone's support to ensure the children have all the love they need. I can't be both parents. I will be the best damn mother I can be, but it truly does take a village, and I am grateful for my village."

Javier took it upon himself to clean up Cher's lounge. All of the information gathered from Joshua's or Antonio's disappearance was placed in files and sealed in a box for Sade. I will hold on to it at our house until Sade is ready to go through everything again.

Cher asked me if I still had time to finalize my designs for Fredricka when I return. Hearing the question brought a smile to my face that lit up my soul. I responded holding everyone's undivided attention.

"What I hadn't intended to discuss tonight was my decision to open my own fashion house. After seeing my design come to fruition, I have decided to remain independent, rather than work for Fredricka. My creativity and my vision are my own. Life is too short to get lost in another person's footprints. I must leave my own."

"Honey I am so proud of you, and I will continue to be here for you every step of the way. It won't be easy, but it will most definitely be worth it." Pierre's voice was filled with tenderness and overwhelmed with love. "Pierre, your love is one of my greatest blessings. I appreciate you so much."

"Where will you design?" Rae asked with a puzzled look on her face. "I will use my home office space and Artistry for now. I am hoping Pierre will be able to help me with ideas on expanding the space at Artistry to include a storefront boutique. So many details left to iron out, but one thing that I am sure of is that I will no longer be working for Fredricka."

Immediately Cher's face lit up. Sounding like she had just won the lottery, her voice was filled with unmasked excitement. "Vic, oh my goodness! I am so happy and excited for you. When I purchased property here, and left my stable job to start my own business I was terrified, yet driven at the same time. There is no greater feeling than being in control of your craft and vision. You have an investor in me, no questions asked. Knowing this is always what I have wanted for you, I pledge right here, right now to donate three million dollars to you for seed money. This way you can plan how you will expand Artistry and have a little cushion to get your designs ready for showing. My wheels are turning. You have to come back to the island soon and check out another property I purchased near the restaurant. You may find it perfect as a second boutique, store-front location."

With tears of joy streaming down my face, I reached for Cher's hands. "Wow, Cher, you never cease to amaze me. I love and appreciate you more than words can ever express." Smiling, while holding my hands in hers, she continued. "Now you know, I am always here for all of you. Somehow, someway, we will all find the strength to move forward, together. As soon as I set a date for the grand opening, I will send you all an invitation. I will have a grand master table set up for the evening for all of you."

Everyone will stay with me on the island the weekend of the opening and we will celebrate right! There will be live music and delicious cuisine. I think it will be a grand opening to remember, and I need each of you here to celebrate this accomplishment with me. Now let's drink to that!"

Dancing and laughing, completely blocking out the last few days, we welcomed the night and peacefulness knowing that nothing is promised. Whatever work is left for us to do, it will still be waiting in the morning.

# Acknowledgements

I would like to take this opportunity to thank my family for their genuine love, support and continued encouragement. Each of you, in your own way, have motivated me to continue pursuing my personal, professional goals.

To my creative accountability partner, and favorite actress, a fierce entrepreneur, C. Hargrove, I thank you for being you. Sisters in life, I appreciate you for embracing my art, and being here along the way to see the stories in my head come alive.

To my best friend of twenty-five years, J. Pittman, I too thank you for your genuine support and encouragement through the years. You are an inspiring woman, and definitely one of my favorite entrepreneurs. Thank you for your straight, no chaser realness. I appreciate you for always reminding me to move confidently, and to pursue my goals vigorously.